I0782156

KINSMAN AVENUE PUBLISHING, INC.
www.kinsmanquarterly.org

© 2025 Kinsman Avenue Publishing, Inc.

Registered with the U.S. Library of Congress

Printed in the United States of America

Winds of Asia

Cover design and illustrations by Monique Franz

Edited by Jack Wolflink
Co-Editors: Monique Franz, Clara Zimban, Wayne Benson Jr., and Radiyah Nouman

Contributing authors and voices of the Asian diaspora:

Alex Van Huynh, Anna Li Stollman, Anton Imbong, Aparna Rajan, Cathy Millangue, Connie Chen, Dea Ratna, Diane Yang, Elina Kumra, Farah Art Griffin, Hannan Khan, Hasanah Mishahal Mansour, Jade Mah-Vierling, Jiang Pu, Jocelyn A Chin, Joy Pepito, Karina Cheah, KC Sisomphone, Lam Ho, Ling Yuan, Linh Truong, Lucy Zhang, Michelle Chen, Mir Aziz, O. Hunt, Rena Johnson, Rishabh Motwani, Sandra Jackson-Opoku, Serrina Zou, Sol Zerrudo, Songyee Park, Tara Lall, Vaswati Das, and Zoe Parrott.

Winds of Asia

Prose & Poetry
of the Asian Diaspora

Edited by Jack Wolflink

Editor's Note

What is an Asian story? When Kinsman Quarterly opened the Winds of Asia award in September 2024, we did not anticipate over 220 entries, each with its own unique answer to the question. Narrowing down those entries to the 35 we will include in the upcoming collection took some effort, but we are delighted with how these stories, essays, and poems have come together. With entries tackling cultures and histories from China, India, the Philippines, Vietnam, Pakistan, Korea, Indonesia, Japan, Bangladesh, and Laos, the inaugural *Winds of Asia* anthology blows in with all the scents and sensations of Earth's largest continent.

What you'll see within the pages of the upcoming anthology is a whirlwind *mélange* of dreams and dashed hopes, mystery and magic, explorations of the many ways ties can bind (for good and ill), and windows into how those ties are spun. In this collection, families, cuisines, and languages twist into each other and into modernity, both inside and outside Asia's nations. Asian characters work hard to both preserve ancient meanings and spin new ones at the bleeding edge of cultural innovation. If there is one thing Asian stories lack, it is stasis.

Asia has always been in dialogue with the world, much as the jet stream that fuels its winds has always flowed across the skies of Europe, Africa, and North America. Therefore, we at Kinsman Quarterly are beyond proud to be able to present this anthology to you as just one glimmering facet of the global reach of Asia's spirits.

— Jack Wolflink, Editor

Family

Self

Place

Gender

Family

Meena

O. Hunt

She was a year younger than me, yet when I was a girl, she seemed like a woman.

It wasn't that she reached puberty earlier than most. If anything, the years of malnourishment probably predating her birth—starting from conception in her poor and sickly mother's womb—had made her far more waifish than an average eleven-year-old. Her clothes, low-quality *salwar* and *kurti*, with once-bright colors faded from overuse and rough washing, weren't what chiefly belied her age either.

Plodding silently behind her mother, going from one house to another mopping floors and cleaning dishes, she didn't have the lightness of foot characteristic of children. She never ran, never frisked. She walked with shoulders hunched, as if they carried on an invisible weight too heavy. Sometimes, she limped like an old woman after being beaten, especially when her wiry legs took too long to recover.

But more than anything, it was her eyes. Darker than the kohl smudged on her already prominent dark circles because of constant sweating, they held suffering too great for her age. A suffering that seemed to have made her soul weary already. As if she had lived a hundred lives, all starting from adulthood, skipping completely over childhood. As if in all of them she was always Meena. The Meena who was an unwanted, unloved girl. The Meena who was always born a *Dalit*.

May wasn't the month one would choose when planning to return to India from Canada. But my parents did just that.

Our home in Calgary, the Rockies a few hours away, Canmore flanked on all sides by peaks that looked like masts of ghost ships in the dark, the grizzlies and the elks, the walk under the Hoodoos, seemed so distant now that they might as well have been residual fragments from a dream. Here, the very air sizzled, and tiny mirages formed on asphalt highways under the relentless glare of the midday summer sun.

Amidst the mugginess and the crowd, our ancestral home, already new to me, started feeling like a homeless shelter with a maid and her daughter working for a major chunk of my afternoons every day. I started resenting their presence, especially the girl's, because once she finished mopping after her mother, she sat and peered into my life for the half hour her mother took to wash utensils by herself.

Every day, I rushed from school, lest Meena rode my new cycle or took something from my Sailor Moon collection. I had caught her eyeing my room with such longing that I was almost sure she'd try to steal something.

My room was designed to resemble an eclectic chamber of every fantasy of mine. Even though the rest of the house was old-fashioned and rustic, my room was the first to get renovated to be as close as possible to the one in Calgary.

For now, my queen-sized bed was Rapunzel-themed. Faux pink ivy that felt softer to touch than the real plant climbed down from the wall to the headboard of my bed to the floor underneath. Woven with golden Sundrop flowers, the ivy resembled Rapunzel's long braid. The rest of the bedding was varying shades of pink.

On one side of my bed was a bookcase with a crystal red rose in a glass dome atop it inspired by *Beauty and the Beast*. There were Sakura suncatchers hanging by the ceiling and the walls were painted to give the entire space an appearance of *Howl's Moving Castle*.

My room was an object of envy and fascination and put me right at the top of the hierarchy in the world of girls. There were so many figurines and expensive show pieces in my room that if Meena stole something, I wouldn't find out for a long time. Yet, a part of me wished she would do just that, so I could find an excuse to tell on her and get her fired. I wanted her to stop coming into my room.

When my best friends from school, Shreya and Kinjal, came for annual festival skit practice, Meena slowed down and took longer to clean my room. She was creeping my friends out by constantly trying to pry into what we were doing. Her eyes sparkled at every small thing as if she had found a gold mine.

Ordinarily, I had gotten used to her by now, but with her unsightly appearance, cringy behaviour that reeked of poverty and classlessness, and the timid smiles she kept giving us as if she was one of us made me feel embarrassed before my friends.

"Who's she?" Shreya asked with evident disgust. She very well knew who Meena was, but she wanted me to call her a maid in front of everyone.

When my friends asked who she was, it wasn't her name or her age or which school she attended that they wanted to know. I of course, took the hint.

"She's our servant's daughter. A maid herself," I replied. "Don't pay her any mind."

"Can you please hurry up and get out? We are doing something important. Something someone illiterate like you wouldn't understand. Or are you expecting an invitation for a tea party or something?" Kinjal chimed in too.

I knew Meena wasn't illiterate. Mamma had also told me how she was a topper even though she barely attended classes, but I didn't want to correct my friend and look uncool by revealing something nice about Meena.

When with my friends, I thought nothing of what happened. But in the evening, when I sat cross-legged near the little temple and lit the lamp in front of *Shiva* and *Krishna's* idols, I thought of Meena.

Though I wasn't too religious, I felt a tinge of shame once I closed my eyes in our prayer room. The three of us were thought to be such good girls, and we were polite and well-behaved everywhere, then why were we so quick to target and bully Meena and that too with relish?

A new understanding dawned on me; cruelty was an itch everyone scratched whenever they got an opportunity, when the target was weak and couldn't retaliate, when there were no consequences.

Had Mamma seen what I did, she would have scolded me a little, but I knew Grandma would rebuke Mamma for trying to lecture me for an insignificant maid, that too a *Dalit* like Meena.

I was supposed to feel comforted by the fact that most adults around me, no, the society itself, had placed Meena at the very bottom. She had no one she could complain to. Even her mother didn't show her an ounce of love or protection, and her mother was treated like a lowlife by many ladies who employed her.

My occasional taunts were well within the acceptable range of behaviour Meena daily faced, so there was no cause for guilt. Yet it was guilt that kept me awake at night.

Let alone steal, Meena never touched anything in my room, and after that day, she apparently learned to curb her habit of throwing those wistful glances as well. It gave me no relief like I'd imagined it to.

I once saw her accidentally drop my plush pillow lying precariously over the edge while mopping. She quickly picked it up and put it back. Her fingers caressed its softness for a moment before she retracted her hand and looked at it as if it was filthy.

As if it was a kind of filth she didn't believe could be washed away by soap and water alone. As if, if she lingered any longer, she would pass it from herself to the pillow, and then to my shiny life.

Though I had known it all along, like a hot spell, the realization that Meena was a year younger than me, that she was just eleven, scorched me.

Between the scullery and my pink-themed room, it was like a portal in the sky closed for her when she stopped looking at my life, and an abyss opened before me when I started looking at hers.

At the tail end of yet another summer, I started awaiting the petrichor that the first showers would bring. The fresh drizzle settled the dust, and enormous black clouds formed on the equatorial sky.

My clothes had gotten smaller and my trinkets, outdated. Those, along with my textbooks, were given to Meena. Her eyes beamed momentarily while receiving my used stuff, but they dimmed again when she remembered something.

What was it?

When the next day she brought something that resembled a wheat sack instead of my old school bag—relatively brand new and far better than anything she ever possessed I was sure—I couldn't help asking, "Why aren't you using the one we gave you yesterday instead of this trash bag?"

I was offended at the thought of our little charity, though not my idea and though only tangentially related to me insofar as it was the item I owned and had lost interest in that was given away, being rejected by her. That she was possibly not grateful enough irked me.

"It was given to Raju. To take to school."

That made me angry, and the target of my anger shifted. I ran to Mamma to complain. "How can Divya give my bag to Raju? It's Meena who cleans my room every day. Mamma, I think each time we give something to Meena, her useless brother takes it. That's not fair."

Mamma probably found my little outburst adorable and patted my head. "Once we give something to someone as a gift or in charity, how they decide to use it among themselves is up to them. It's still good karma on our part, and we'll be rewarded for it. Besides, we give your clothes and sandals too to Meena and am sure Raju can't use those."

Though Mamma tried to convince me we had done something admirable, I still felt as if we were doing it just to be in the gods' good graces; as if we cared nothing for who the recipient of those tiny acts of benevolence was. As if we were just trying to trick *Ishwar* into thinking we were pious and good people with as little an effort as was comfortably expendable.

If Meena didn't even own a proper bag, I wondered what she took to school. I knew Meena went to a public school in her locality, but I still couldn't help but ask why her school allowed her to take so many leaves.

Meena flinched each time someone asked her a question that required an answer. I had a feeling she preferred being given twenty new commands asking her to do unpaid extra work than being asked anything about her life.

"I go to give exams." Meena weighed every word as she looked at Divya. She tried to be as silent, occupy as little space as possible. And when talking became unavoidable, she kept it brief and always looked at Divya before and after speaking.

Sometimes, though Divya didn't do anything to her in front of us, I later saw her pulling Meena's twig-like arm when she supposedly misspoke, dragging her home while slapping and pinching till they disappeared beyond the gates of our complex.

"My younger son Raju goes to school daily." Divya proclaimed proudly soon after. Every bit of labor and sacrifice on the sister's part seemed to be justified for her brother's shot at a better life.

"You send your boy to school, but not your girl? It's an era of equality, Divya. A girl's education is just as important as the boy's." Mamma lectured solemnly, with a passionate outburst of indignation for a situation she hardly had a clue about minutes ago.

"My husband decides. And Meena scores well even if she doesn't go regularly, so she doesn't need to."

"Isn't your husband unemployed and an alcoholic? Yet you let him make all the decisions?" Mamma scolded.

"He's the man of the house." Divya declared matter-of-factly, then started talking about his alcoholism and unemployment just the same.

It was only when people like Divya talked about the ills of their lot that dignified, richer ladies lent them a patient listening ear. Mamma had to obey Papa and his mother as well. Live her life as per their rules, customs, sometimes even whims. When she listened to Divya, she probably could believe she had it so much better.

It was also strictly one-sided. There was a tacit agreement in the house that Mamma should and could never vent her woes out aloud or be called out in front of those she considered infinitely below her own station.

For Divya and Meena, Mamma was a master. A more patient, good-natured one than many others, but still someone they were in no position to pity even if they stopped working for us.

After all, till the day we die, we'll belong to the upper caste, and they to one of the lowest. Even if they become millionaires and we go bankrupt, that, just like our blood type, won't change.

I didn't know much about the caste system back in Calgary, except when grandma asked about my Indian friends' surnames over calls and warned me against befriending a few of them. I never understood what it was about surnames then, what was she trying to determine about a person by knowing just their last name, but I was slowly grasping it now.

With my old book, Meena sat cross-legged on the cold tiled floor, aloof from everything around. Even though she was usually silent unless asked, there was something about her presence I couldn't ignore. It reminded me of the Zen monks I'd once seen.

Was it a coping mechanism? Resilience? Something qualitatively different about her soul? I couldn't understand.

I sidled up to her. "Why do you study so hard? What do you want to be?"

"I want to earn enough so that if I have a daughter, she won't have to work while she's young. A government job would be good."

That was all Meena said on the matter, and for once, she didn't look at Divya for her approval.

By the time Grandma came to stay with us for a few months, Meena had taken over most of her mother's work. She was alone under Grandma's disapproving scrutiny.

When Grandma came, everyone acted differently. Mamma stepped down from her position as the mistress of the house for a few months and turned meeker in front of Grandma. Mamma, who was otherwise sympathetic and kind to Meena, asked her about her studies, gave her my barely used stationery items and clothes—stopped most of that during Grandma's stay.

Whether it was the fear of her mother-in-law, or a desire to avoid conflicts with Papa by being in his mother's good books, or just a desire to impress the matriarch of the family, Mamma turned colder to Meena.

Grandma had been disappointed in Mamma for not trying for a boy when Mamma miscarried after me. Though that was many years ago in the past, I thought Mamma didn't want to give any more reasons to Grandma to be disappointed. Grandma now treated me like her princess and loved me just as much, if not more, than she loved Papa.

I loved her but I sometimes wondered if I would have been as important and as beloved as I was now if I had a brother. I had seen Kinjal being ordered around by her mother to do her brother's bidding.

If guests came, the mother and the daughter served everyone while the father and the brother ate with the guests first. When her brother came home from school, and if her mother was unavailable, it was my friend's duty to cater to her brother; serve him food and clean the table after he was finished.

And it was only worse in poorer households like Meena's. That was probably why Meena's freedom and childhood being sacrificed while her brother being treated like a prince to the extent their circumstances allowed, made my blood boil whenever I heard Divya talk.

As for Grandma, I wondered how someone who was so loving to a few people could be so hateful to someone so young and wholly innocent. Grandma held too many contradictions, and old age calcified them in a way they could no longer be fixed. Or maybe she was always like that—I couldn't tell.

She noticeably held Meena's lot in contempt. Yet she'd rather they work for us than let Mamma buy a dishwasher or a vacuum cleaner instead. Grandma did have compassion; it wasn't fake, but limited and selective.

When she called girls from poorer neighborhoods for meals during the festival of *Navratri* and gave them pretty gifts afterwards, Meena, whom we had known for years, who worked for us, who was trustworthy enough to leave our house keys with when we all went out, was never one of them.

If someone was poor, and from an upper caste, especially a *Brahmin*, their poverty had dignity to it. It was even commendable, in an idealistic sort of way.

Grandma funded fees and books for our upper caste cook's twins even though they barely visited, and even though the cook was only called when Mamma was out or sick. Yet, when Meena was given my old books, and when Mamma forgot to act cold and praised Meena for her academic success despite circumstances, Grandma was almost livid.

"It must be the reservation quota."

When I explained that's not how it was in Meena's case, and that she was in the top three, Grandma was ready with an argument about why that was no achievement at all.

"Well, of course she can score high if the class is filled with people like *them*. Just like their teachers. They set up easy tests and give high scores to anyone and his dog."

Meena tried avoiding Grandma's gaze and taunts as she went about her work. But on a Sunday afternoon, I made a blunder that cost Meena her job.

"Mamma, why can't Meena cook for us? She makes her tiffin. I once had a bite from her *paratha*. She'll make more money cooking and she's better than—"

Before I could finish, I heard Grandma shout.

"Girl! Girl!"

We all knew she wasn't calling me. I heard a steel pan clang, and Meena came running.

"Did you try to feed my child?" Grandma looked at Meena as if she'd pull her by her hair and smash her against the wall.

"She didn't offer…anything. I just took…had a little morsel because it smelled good." I tried to sound firm, but I was hardly audible.

"She wants to corrupt my house. My child. Vile girl! Get out. Now!"

"But mother—" Mamma tried to reason, but Grandma cut her off.

"It's me or her in this house."

Grandma was hyperventilating.

Mamma gave Meena three months' worth of wages. Other than some extra cash, there wasn't much Mamma could do even if she felt bad.

Meena's eyes seemed to cry without tears that she wasn't allowed to shed.

As for me, I had to spend half a day purifying myself with the water from the Ganges and sitting in the prayer room as penance. When I came out, Grandma was composed again.

"You cannot eat food made by *Dalits*. Fleeing to another country for a few years doesn't give you a license to act ignorant and profane yourself. But it's not your fault you weren't taught better." Grandma looked at Mamma bitterly.

"We can't treat them as *untouchables* in this day and age, Grandma. The Indian Constitution bans it and it doesn't feel right, anyway."

"We tolerate them in our house, give them jobs, and that's still not enough? We must let them sully everything sacred? Is your constitution above *Karmic law*? They are *Dalits* in this life because of their sins in the previous one. What you think is their suffering is divine justice."

"Then we'll also be *Dalits* in the next life for our sins against them in this one?"

I felt a sharp sting on my cheek. For the first time, Grandma had slapped me. Mamma came rushing, but my eyes were too blurry to see what unfolded next.

Grandma was deeply hurt and left in a week. We exchanged no hugs or goodbyes.

When the old tenants moved out, a new family shifted right in front of us. The patriarch of the house, the older Mr. Dubey, was a friendly man by all appearances. They hired Meena to look after his grandson. The man seemed kind at first. It turned out he was fond of Meena. Maybe a little too fond.

I only ever saw her working from afar till we left for Calgary again. She'd started draping a thick *dupatta*. I thought I saw bruising on her neck from my window when her *dupatta* slipped down once. Her parents hit her, but not on the neck. Never on the neck.

Apparently, she was considered *untouchable* no longer when it came to this.

Once the old man's wife came back from her older son's house, Meena was fired. A seductress, a slut, and a 'fallen woman' were her new descriptors, among others. She was fifteen then.

I heard rumors from old neighbors over calls. Because of the scandal, Meena was married off to a man more than twice her age as soon as she turned eighteen. The man had an infant daughter and a son almost as old as Meena.

The old Dubey and his wife initially considered a divorce, but because of intervention from the rest of the family, their decades-long marriage was saved.

"My husband is an otherwise upstanding man who won't do such a thing if it wasn't for that girl being a whore. Then again, what else can you expect from such low-class women? Richer, unsuspecting men are their targets. Besides, it's all grossly exaggerated. He barely touched her after she repeatedly tried seducing him at his lowest. Otherwise, who'd even look at that thing?"

Mrs. Dubey helped restore her husband's good reputation. Everyone agreed people deserve second chances. Unless if they were Meena. He became the community head in a few years. Meena wasn't seen in that neighborhood again.

⚶

I walked through the quagmire; amid fetid odor from overflowing gutters, I couldn't smell the soft fragrance of wet soil, nor pay attention to the majestic gray clouds forming above as I focused on avoiding the puddles below.

There was hardly any beauty to the monsoon in the slums. I now understood why Meena once said she hated the season that I loved from my cozy window. I'd considered her too crass to enjoy the romance of the rains then.

Outside the squalor of the slums, a small house stood on a mound. The scent of sandalwood wafted from it, probably from an incense stick. I climbed and peered inside for a minute. It looked cleaner and sturdier than others around. A few flowers were potted along the small window, used containers patched and painted to create the pots.

I knocked hesitantly. "Meena?"

Would she recognize me soon? It was likely a wrong decision, but something had brought me here that I didn't quite understand.

A cute girl who looked almost as old as Meena when I'd first met her opened the door. She had a *mogra* in her braid and wore a neat pink frock with a vivid floral print on it. Her palms had no calluses. Her brown eyes were unbothered and dreamy. Her face was ruddy.

Meena stepped out from behind her. Though she was surprised to see me, she recognized me at once and smiled.

"Your step-daughter?"

Meena nodded. The girl circled Meena's waist and hid her face shyly in the folds of her mother's *dupatta*. From time to time, she peeked to look at me and grinned. Meena caressed her head and said, "My daughter, Nisha."

Meena had started going to college after her husband's death. Even though she couldn't resume her studies any sooner, she worked as a seamstress to send Nisha to a private school. Meena never had children of her own.

When I first inherited Grandpa's real estate, I thought I was coming here to offer Meena a job as the manager of the estate. Something far more lucrative and preferable for her, hopefully, than working as a seamstress. Besides, I was, in a way, responsible for her losing her job all those years ago.

But a lump formed in my throat when I tried to speak out everything I thought I would tell her when we met.

"I am sorry."

That was all I could manage to mumble. Sorry for all my intentional and unintentional cruelties toward her. Sorry for everything she suffered in our household.

For a while, all we shared was silence. Did she want to say she accepted my apology, that I was a child at the time too? Or did she want to curse me and say she hated me all that while, and hates me now for coming here?

With some hesitance, she extended her hand. What for? What did you want to say, Meena? But before I could react, she pulled it back out of long ingrained fear as if I was still a shiny thing she couldn't sully.

Meanwhile, Nisha came out with food on her plate. It was a familiar fragrance.

"It's dinnertime and I'm hungry. Would you, perhaps, let me eat a *paratha* or two? Only if there are any leftovers, of course."

I used to keep throwing questions at her whenever I got a chance, and she was nervous every single time before answering. But to ask this one required all the strength I could muster.

"*Can* you?" She asked back meaningfully.

"Can I help you make it, you mean? I may not be as good as you, but I have recently learned some cooking. Let me show you."

When Meena brushed my hand despite cautiously handing me the rolling pin, I took her hands in mine and pressed them softly. Her hands were cold, and so were mine. I held them long enough for both of ours to get warm.

"About what you said earlier, it's okay," she said. I think this was the first time I saw Meena smile; a beautiful smile full of melancholy.

I wanted to ask if she had found some moments of happiness, if she could find any semblance of kindness in this world. I wanted to ask if her husband was any better to her, if her parents finally saw her worth.

When I looked at Nisha, I had a feeling that everything Meena lacked in her life was given to Nisha tenfold. I couldn't imagine what was required of a woman to be able to create a happy childhood for a child that wasn't even her own flesh and blood when she had never known happiness herself. But I knew it was something beyond what I could ever achieve.

I hadn't expected to stay for that long, but upon Meena and Nisha's insistence, I ended up staying after dinner too. I was afraid she'd not want to see me or anyone from that part of her life. I searched her eyes. They reflected fatigue and brokenness—from poverty, from cruelty, from every injustice of life. Yet, there was no hint of malice or hostility in them. There never was.

I fully understood in that moment what I envied and was in awe of in childhood but could find no words for at the time, and the more I grasped the immensity of Meena's strength of character, the more I regretted it probably not being acknowledged by anyone.

After a while, Nisha was comfortable enough to show me her brand-new cycle, her books, the medals she had gotten in sports and in singing. She revealed she wanted to be a singer and a songwriter. She had written a few songs, many of them referencing or dedicated to her mother.

In Nisha's carefree smiles and songs, her frequent trips within the small room to go to her mother before coming back to show me one more thing, I could sense the reward Meena seemed to have gotten from her trial of a life.

The chairs were flimsy and creaked under our weights when we laughed, but the sound of our laughter drowned those grating sounds.

Even with mellow lights, the room was bright enough for me to see, and I saw no portals or abysses. The place I was in felt only like a home.

Daughter Diaspora

Poetry Collection

Serrina Zou

Serrina Zou

Mothering

after Annie Cao

My daughter can 飞. This, because in her poems
she reaches for wings I do not remember flitting

from my womb. She touches 天, two heavens stitched by our shared
body. Mist dissolves in her tea

leaf palms, fertile sleep in her lifelines. I read
her palms once and knew her before she knew

this future. She thinks I don't pay attention
to the fever scribbles at the margins of her calculus:

her infinity curls into cuffs, the ones I leash to her.
When she disappears into the parchment-white walls

of all her better lives, I shuffle her zodiac charts
like Mahjong tiles, our signs incompatible like the war

-worn halves of 中文 and 英语. The latter, a salted light
yolked into our eggs. My English is not good.

Early in ESL class, I chewed nouns in the order of operations: mother
(singular) + daughter (singular) = family (singular).

Grammar, a grieving calculation. My math knows
this love better. She will not know the limits of

chrysanthemums and sea songs, rotting sunbeams shying the secrets
between us. How they clawed me

home to her. This life, a divergence test she rams
with her goat horns the way I peck rice grains

with my rooster beak. She writes me
and loves me like a crowing villain. I know she is lonely.

She wants proofs cast in gold, churched salvation,
an adoption of lightning, but no love, no husband, no me.

Under my sweat-shingled roof of 家,
I am feathering the English to help her soar.

Poem Written in the Jade Palace Bathroom

If I was the empress, I wouldn't question this fantasy:

my eight selves sauntering these walls, dragonflies

dotting the sea glass stalls. I drink Tuesdays

in cocktails crafted with a slurry of cranes

the last daughter pinned with the bartender's

number. My empress, he grins, as if willing

a wealth of sons between his ivory teeth. In this bathroom

devouring dynasties, I watch our children trail ink-dipped

beards into the sink, the beginnings of poems.

When they wed wives cut from my crown jewels,

I tell them the truth: I never dreamt a red chamber,

only this jade prison where snakes bloom across the dais.

Serrina Zou

Ghazal of Light
for Auntie Indira

If light is in your heart, you will find your way home.
—Rumi

In chai-steamed November, my godmother swaths me
in her iridescent saris, quiets my light
protests. Her eyes, gauzy with mischief, shimmer
as if to welcome this festival of light.

Outside, the sky scatters into a thousand fireworks.
The wind sweeps through our skin, warm
despite autumn's dying breath. My godmother squeezes my
hand against flickering tealights.

I ask her if the gods will forgive me. *For what, chutki?*
Her clipped English falls away, Hindi
 sweetening the air in sprinkles of rosewater, saffron,
cardamom. A mirage of delight

honeyed across the kitchen altar. *For loving*
you more than my own blood mother. For loving
the sharp laughter & spice of this holiday more
than the subdued silence of moonlight

during tight-lipped Lunar New Year dinners in Shanghai
where daughters muffle entire shrines with their shouts.
For loving family more than
filial piety. In the dimming candlelight

my fingertips trace voyages across the Pacific,
racing my godmother. This is a journey she
remembers with a smile the way my mother remembers
my scowl. The albums highlight

the year 1998 when my mother wilts in
a borrowed red qipao. My godmother unfurls her
wedding lehenga like a blushing bride.
Their dresses: lotus petaled with enlightenment

shy silk unraveling. My godmother's fingers, bone nimble
from years of threading fate into
freedom, outpace mine. In the distance
between us, I tremble under the house lights.

She cups my cheeks with her milk-soft palms.
There is enough love in this life as there is light.
This time, I don't protest, only nod. Looking up
I find our faces awash with feasts of light.

The Chinese Rapunzel

When my mother braids my hair
                      she destroys the estranged history of us.
Through valleys of tangles and tassels
                      whispering soft *shrr shrr* sounds,
she slurs cricket tunes into violence
                      no daughter can unwind.
In the attic, she grips the shears
                      to my midnight rivers,
murders thirteen years of combing
                      and camphor prayers in one fell swoop
the way I imagine her revolution
                      took her body
and her mother's body before that.
                      This language she wept an ocean
to cleanse my daughter tongue
                      bears no room for plurality:

there is no space for second chances.
                Two years ago the supple ends
my native rope split along itself,
                fraying on the noose of its unarmored shaft.
The daughter strands: thinner, softer.
                I considered staving off their hunger
in the same medical procedure
                where I was taught to splice my name:
on the jagged teeth of my DNA helix,
                the legacy coiling in my broken bones.
When drafting her will, my mother leaves me
                nothing save for a debt she absconded
on the night her maidenhood was to die.
                The story of surrender is so sterile:
she sings it to me like a church hymn—
                she, the fallen aristocrat's daughter,
boned into waitress and wife clothes.
                and twenty-five years later, the hairs she braid
is the only inheritance that does not
                limn daughter into marauder.
Like my mother's daughter, I learn
                learn too late to thieve light
from our litany of loss—unravel this genome of lies.

On the Flight into my Future, I Refuse my Dreams.

after K-Ming Chang

        My funeral shroud arrives
in sleep—pale horizon pink
        knifing away leftovers

of yesterday's bleary warmth.
        I soften the sky's edges
with my tears, let stars flicker

in my sockets. Dimming daughters
waiting to burn out. In the heavens,
        everything spins. and I still

the window shades, tell my mother
        the weather forecast for arrival: bright,
blistering heat. A grinning god.

        My earliest astronomy lesson:
the sun is the brightest star
        visible on earth. A flare

searing our irises with the shapes
        of simpler times. At the reading of my will I
conceive my mother's spirit

quoting Lao Tzu, her favorite philosopher: the flame that
        burns twice as bright burns half as long the way she
forewarned me the day I dyed

my eyes the loneliest blue, an omen
        to preface the most beautiful part of my body. To
predict where it was headed.[1]

        My mother spoke in pearls that day:
little aphorisms of pellucid light.
        I was to believe the world

was my oyster so long as I could swallow her sand.
        Long enough to string the sky
into the sea & call it flight. During landing,

        three hours beyond the west,
I drench my skin in nighttide, waiting
        for the sky to turn.

[1] From "Someday I'll Love Ocean Vuong" by Ocean Vuong

Kaingin

[kah-ING-in]

Sol Zerrudo

Fire turns everything to dust. But as you leave the land to fallow, in the shadow of the violent blaze, is life to be nurtured.

The man knew of fire; he knew its importance, of its power. It takes with cruel apathy, yet it gives selflessly. Abundance, destruction—all in the same plane as his gods intended. "Oh, gods," he whimpered, on his knees in despair. "My gods, have you abandoned me?" Shoulders slumped, tears misting his vision, in the man's eyes was a reflection of his house in flames. They grew brighter each second; midnight sun illuminating the mountainous ridge he and his people call home.

The man stared at the simmering inferno, unseeing, nearly blinded. He whispered to himself in a trance:

They've done it. They've done it.

The lowlanders have come. And they've come to *take*."

For decades, they've coveted the lush ancestral lands of his people – the *Sulud*. The crops grew larger where the nomadic Sulud stayed; the rice was more fragrant, and the harvest profuse. The wildlife flourished along with it, seemingly never-ending.

The man's ancestors shared the land's bounty, believing it would bring peace. And as they did, the lowlanders grew in numbers, put up fences, and demanded sole ownership of what should belong to everyone created by the gods *Laki* and *Bayi*.

Now they had come to claim the rest of what isn't theirs by blood, through *fire*. The man wept and his tears mixed with the warm earth. Billowing draughts of hot air caressed his skin like a swab. His lips trembled.

❧

His neighbors from the nearby mountain came. They brought with them pots of water from the riverbank, passed them along to each other in an orderly fashion, and heaved its contents to the fire. The flames licked back and sizzled, whistling, smoke enveloping the surroundings.

26

The man didn't move. His knees stayed grounded to the soil, pebbles digging into his skin.

Through the commotion, someone shook his shoulders to ask him a question: "Where are your sons?!"

The man's gaze sharpened. His mouth fell wide and he let out a pained howl. His house, his wives, his children…

The people around him knew then: the man had just lost everything.

Pasanon ta't turoson

Na patawasa't tarangison

Let's leave him whimpering

Wailing the fear of his heart

Bansagun, the elder, chanted the epic Hinilawod. The children around him listened as he sang, his voice a soothing trill. The man listened intently as Bansagun told the story of the goddess Alunsina, who after marrying a mortal and giving birth, offered *alanghiran* fronds and *kamangyan* incense to the fire for her sons' health.

At the mention of the incense, the man burst into tears once again and interrupted Bansagun, albeit momentarily. The elder gave the man a kind stare and sat with him gently through his sorrow.

The man buried his sons with the best funeral clothes he could find— all red, intricately handwoven *panubok* made by the last kept maiden in the area. He laid their remains beside their mothers, buried them where the sun first kisses the earth as it rises, as proof of his devotion.

But he could not bathe them in kamangyan. He could not pour the ginger and mountain herb concoction over their small bodies, nor perfume them so that they may appease the evil spirits who devour the dead in Muruburu.

The man sobbed harder. The lowlanders knew about the Sulud culture of death. Fire is meant for sacrifices, offerings, and for cultivation. It is not meant for the souls. How despicable the lowlanders are to rob his family of a peaceful descent into the underworld. Even in death, they made sure that he could never be reunited with them again.

His heart ached; through the pain, the man's insides grew ablaze.

Imaw gida'y ginsugdan	*For this is the beginning*
Nga imaw gid ginpunon-an	*Of the incident that tells*
Ka bukadyong Tarangban	*The story of Tarangban*
Nga bukay nga Kurundalan	*Of the Stone-walled Kurundalan*

If his gods would not allow him to reunite with his loved ones, maybe the gods of the lowlanders would.

He'd heard stories about how the lowlanders' god forgave those who had done wrong—how their god welcomed all, and made their desires come true in a place called 'heaven'. The man knew what he wanted in heaven.

Maybe he could make a vow. He could make a vow to put down his sharp *sanduko*. He would take off the *pulos* on his head, vow to abandon the *diwatas*, and forget his life as a Suludnon. Quickly, the man went back to his brother-in-law's house. He wrapped his red scarf around his head, tied his weapon around his waist. His eyes glittered with tears. He was born beloved by the Sulud gods, his parents said, but he would give up his faith in his deities for a chance to reunite with his family.

The man bid the last of his people farewell and turned his back to Bansagun, who chanted the last of Hinilawod, the verses cautioning the hero crossing the sea.

Kun magsalakay kamo mamkaw	*When you journey across the waters Let forth in*
Magkapyo kag mangayow	*in faraway seas*
Kag hindon niny mangyan	*And you happen to pass by*
Ada masapgiranan	*And come near the coast*
Buyong buot kaw tigamhan	*Lord, be cautious, be wary*
Kaspan, karuhun-ruhon	*Be very careful*

But it would not be water he would be facing in his journey.

It would take the man a day of walking to reach the town where the lowlanders lived. And when he finally does: The man brings with him only a container of kerosene and a single matchstick. He will abandon his gods, but first, the lowlanders must pay.

They will pay through fire and blood.

His gods would understand. After all, they were the ones who had taught the Sulud: "Cut down and burn, and from the charred soil may the earth yield its bounty tenfold."

餃子
JiaoZi
(Dumpling)

Connie Chen

onsider the dumpling. They covered your eyes but forgot your ears. The pig that you named and fed for a year with your leftovers screams at its slaughter. The hose that tangled around your feet every time you filled its trough is uncoiled, stretching to spit on the splatters of blood staining the cement sty. The sweating spine, ripened on the rice made every day on that very stove and on the morsels chewed by that very cleaver, sinks unflinchingly into the boiling bath to milk its marrow. The bubbling storm of star anise, cloves, ginger, cinnamon, and sun-dried mandarin peels rise in futile rebellion. The Auntie in the brown, sauce-stained apron wanted more belly fat and you watch the ankles and shoes and the red socks peeking through shuffle across the kitchen, dripping rusty liquid, veining on the floor.

You fell for the snowfall wedding the world around the dining table, and the fingers that made it fall—light and even over the deep walnut grains lost in the slow sifting flour. Five rolling pins at the table treaded hoods of dough, enchanted by the circular path—around and around the pillowy center. Another hand of another Auntie separated your minced friend into two mixing bowls: pickled cabbage, garlic, *more garlic*, ginger, *more ginger*, scallions, *more scallions*; chives, *more chives*, garlic, *a little more, that's enough*, shrimp, *just a little more broth*. And we dug our fingers into the pile of white pepper and five spice darkening under the soy and sesame oil, kneading and beating the dead beast into a slurry.

The assembly line from the wrappers to the wrapping was oiled by gossip. "And how's the new boss?"

"Did she really?"

"Look at your cousin! You need to get your shit together."

"I know, I know…"

One chopstick full of filling, jammy with the juicy promise of land and sea, glistened in the center of the wrapper cradled in the knuckles of my left hand. We dipped our ring fingers into the water dish and wetted the upper lips of our dumplings—articulating the mileage of miracles over our fingertips' prayer—pinching at the cupid's bow, pleating and tucking in this year's seeking and sacrifice, kissing the sweat and sunlight and secrets sealed from one end to the other, from this year to the next.

For last year's work belongs to last year's belly, and next year's work awaits another beast—to root at the pig sty, in the soil, and by the shore, every dawn awaiting the fishing boats; to name and kill new friends, to chew and digest who and what and how you love.

Our white pregnant purses tender to the touch line up for labor by the stove and the hands that mothered the ladle pointed out the window and covered my ears. The night sky screamed at the scorching fire taking root at its zenith, blooming into red chrysanthemums rapidly aborting, scarring the heavens with iridescent gasps at this one dangerous life.

Big River Crossing
and Dirty Dozens

Sandra Jackson-Opoku

This plot may be unmarked, yet folks seem to know who I am.

"Ain't Sam Sam yonder up the hill?" They shade their eyes against the sun and point like they can see me. "First Chinese in Elmwood Cemetery."

To be the first of anything makes for a lonely existence. Though I may have died easy, I do not rest that way. Honored reader, please indulge an old man's reminiscences.

Before Clifford Mellis became my father-in-law, he spoke of death as a crossing-over. "Bronze John has took my wife, Mr. Sam. Verity crossed over just the other morning."

Like a debt it forgot to collect, that rascal yellow fever soon returned for Mr. Mellis.

The Chinese look at death as a journey to the underworld, while Colored people see it as a bridge, with the living settled on one side of the water and dead folks on the other. I imagine it something like Big River Crossing that separates two Memphis cities—one big and bustling, the other small and sleepy.

When the air is warm and the wind is high, I can almost hear the Mississippi sighing three miles to the west. Maybe those waters bring whispers from the living. Maybe they aren't sighs but sobs, lamenting my friendless state.

Elmwood seems a fitting resting place since I have always lived near water. I remember first the Pearl of my childhood, the river junks, and sampans of tea and spices going out, the opium coming in. You could smell the reeking loads from a mile away.

Where water courts the riverbank with pearl-polished shells.

It seems I was fated for a solitary life. Could it be in the blood?

My honored mother was the seventh child of a poor rice farmer. I never addressed her as "Mah," never knew her given name. Like everyone else, I called her "younger sister."

Mui-Mui never grew to woman size. I was taller than my mother even as a young boy. I do not remember the Chinese word for it, but in English, they call this type of person a dwarf.

Mui-Mui's birth family lived like many country people. Generations of tenant farmers grew and harvested rice, paying rent and taxes on land they would never own. Looking back, I can see it was like sharecropping, a step away from slavery.

One year, the crop failed, and Mui-Mui's father struggled to feed his family. He went to the market and sold off his youngest, the one he thought too small and weak for work. My mother remembered standing in the village square where pigs and oxen were auctioned.

The man who bought her was a spice merchant, cruel as any cotton planter. Mui Mui served his wife and cared for his children, no matter that she was a child herself. Who would have thought her weak, the way my mother worked? She cooked, cleaned, and childminded by day and made goods for the merchant's trade at night. Mui-Mui hardly slept.

Her master became my father in the expected way.

"The man would have me every night right under the family roof." The tears Mei-Mei held for years she shed when we fled our captivity. "A merchant is a man without shame. He is one step above a slave, one step below a farmer."

Would my honored mother lose face if she knew her only son became a merchant, too?

Mui Mui and I followed the river down to Guangzhou. We came there to meet no one, and no one came to meet us. How odd to feel alone in this big, bustling capital. A city full of foreigners had rechristened it Canton.

A delta churning wide and brackish, gathering itself to join the sea.

Chinese was an old place, but the Pearl was yet young, deep-running, and impetuous. It may have been my first river, but it would not be my last.

We duped ourselves into thinking we'd be safe, and for a time, we were. Then death came calling from across the river. Opium had made us the "Sick Men of Asia." The emperor forbade foreigners from bringing us this drug, and when they refused, we fought a war and were defeated.

We not only lost face in the aftermath, we also lost our seaports. With the Union Jack flying above Canton, strangers came in larger numbers, roaming the outer city with their Chinese emissaries. They bartered opium for trade goods—porcelain, tea, silver, and our people.

When my honored mother died, I was no longer a boy but not yet a man. Unmoored from my anchor stone and lonelier than ever, I fell into a riptide they called the "coolie trade." It pulled me out to sea in my first crossing over, a water wider than any river, and saltier than tears.

I knew I would die in the overseas so I never tried to find my way back home. Before I came to rest at Elmwood, my life ebbed and flowed with the river currents. Yet these were new places and strange waters.

Mississippi, Big Muddy.

Broad and dark as a buffalo's back.

A man of the Chinese South came to toil in the American South. Before arriving, I never knew bondage was newly ended. White bosses tried to replace Colored with Asian labor. My honored mother had been enslaved, and now it seemed that I was too.

I was badly used in the cane fields of Louisiana and cotton fields of Mississippi—beaten, overworked, starved, cheated. They worked Chinese like the slaves before us, but there was a difference. They bossed but couldn't buy us. When a situation displeased me, I could turn away and cross the nearest river.

I heard of a place named for the city and river I'd left behind. Chinese believe in fateful signs, so I thought this might be a lucky arrival. I now realize I was rushing from one solitude to another.

A sleepy stream of sluggish brown alligators riding her coattails.

Just as the Pearl of Guangdong stretches toward the delta, the Pearl of Mississippi empties into the Sound. Otherwise, drowsy little Canton was nothing at all like Guangzhou.

It traded in cotton, vast fields of it growing on the outskirts. My friendships were few and fleeting. The Coloreds were browbeaten, the White folks cruel, and I never met another Chinese in all my time there. After sharecropping for only a season, I knew I wouldn't stay.

I followed the Pearl down to Jackson, where I found crews building the Yazoo and Mississippi Valley Railroad. By then I was no longer a young man but my body still was strong.

I got hired on as a spiker in a crew they called "The Chinaman Gang." Some of us did not like this word but I will not argue against it. I am Chinese, and also a man. Not celestial monkey, bamboo coon, or chink.

Yazoo, child of the Tallahatchie and Yalobusha, rushing to meet the Mississippi.

We followed gandy dancers along the line, pounding in spikes to tighten rails to the track. Backbreaking but steady work, it paid better than picking cotton and chopping cane.

Our crews ironed the road to Yazoo City and then beyond it. We linked the Y&MV onto the old Yazoo Delta line, the one they called the Yellow Dog. Creeping steadily northward, the men camped in woods and along bayous, laying rails and blasting out culverts as we went.

The bossman paid the rain, wind, and cold no-never-mind. Railroad workers never rested out the weather. Panthers, bears, and alligators roamed those parts. We caught and ate of them before they could catch and eat of us.

Some poor Whites saw a Black or Chinese man with a dollar in his pocket as a threat to their manhood and a temptation to their womenfolk. They swept into our camps with flaming brands, even attacking White laborers who got in their way. Men were beaten, sometimes killed. Ties were burned, the draft horses stolen or slaughtered. It got to where the railroad began sending armed guards to protect their workers and property.

Instead of following the river's flow, I'd been moving against it, struggling upstream like a spawning paddlefish. By the time the Yazoo and Mississippi Valley Railroad met the Illinois Central Line, I had tired of physical labor and the harsh solitudes of backwoods living

Though I was born in the countryside, I'd been raised in the city. I wanted to feel those rhythms again. I left the railroad to become a shopkeeper, opening Sam Sam's Grocery in an old storage shed along the edges of Orange Mound.

A wife awaited me there in Memphis, though neither of us knew at the time.

❧

"Do not forget, Miss Angeline." I wrapped fatback in butcher paper, weighed out the cornmeal, and tucked it into her handbasket. "You are six months late on your grocery bill."

"You think I don't know that, Mr. Sam? You'll get your money, I promise you."

She took the handbasket and rustled away. Angeline's full skirts swayed like she was dancing.

"You are Mr. Clifford's girl," I called after her. "I am trusting you for it."

I offered my customers credit for a small fee, though I expected the bill to be settled each month. If not, I cut them off until their account was clear. Yet I was willing to give this girl grace.

Angeline Mellis, unlike some, was never one to beg, grovel, or play on anyone's pity. She was penniless but proud. Her father, Clifford, had been a hard-working man before he fell sick. He always settled his bill on time, and treated everyone fairly—the Colored, the White, and Chinese.

Times were hard for all of us. Yellow fever took a steamship up from New Orleans. Then Bronze John went stomping through Memphis, kissing everyone he met on the lips. Folks died so quickly Elmwood could not bury them fast enough.

Angeline Mellis was a second-year student at Clay Street School when she left to nurse her ailing family. They sickened and crossed over one by one until she was the last one standing.

Though Angeline never finished her schooling, the girl was far more educated than I. She was also too young for me, but I wanted her anyway. She wouldn't let me court her until she'd paid the last penny on her account.

"Let no man say he bought Angeline Mellis for the price of a grocery bill."

She said we clanged together like two loose pennies in the pocket of a pair of overalls. No one stood up for us but grocery shop customers and the ghosts of fallen family.

Yet our marriage brought the luck I'd been chasing all my life. Yellow fever packed its bags and moved to other parts. Angeline Sam was the charm to make life sweet and a business prosper. She filled my heart with happiness and our house with family, though we also suffered sadness.

Wǔ, 五, the Chinese word for five, can seem like the sound of weeping. Our fifth child died in the cholera plague, though the other four survived to have children of their own.

When I finally crossed over, hundreds came to pay respects at Sam Sam's Grocery Shop. I was carried to Elmwood by my twenty-four descendants, a number that means "easy to die."

Yet, I do not rest easy here. I am forever lonely in this village of the dead. Other Chinese ghosts have come to join me, and the living place flowers at my grave. All of them are strangers I never knew in life.

When the air is warm and the wind is high the voices come. Is it Angeline calling from Elmwood's Colored section or the Mississippi sighing from Big River Crossing?

Dirty Dozens

"What the hell is she saying?" I whispered hotly. "Did that woman just call me a whore?"

Lotus Petal had stormed into our Friday night show at the Black Cat Club, facing the bandstand and shouted me down. Père Prettiman, the bandleader, had learned some Mandarin during his years in Shanghai. He was laughing so hard he could barely translate, but I got the gist of it. I, Luz Acosta Lee, was nothing short of a dusky man-stealing wench.

I lifted my hand and Pére signaled the band to pause. Ming, the nightclub manager, hovered discreetly in the shadows. He'd signal the Russian bouncer if things got out of hand.

"Well, look who's hustling tricks tonight," I called into the sudden silence. "Baby, this is a jazz club, not a house of ill repute. Slim pickings on the Garden Bridge tonight, little flower?"

"Walking the Garden Bridge" was weasel-words for streetwalking, the lowest form of prostitution. It was the worst you could call any courtesan who prized herself as a high-class consort and professional entertainer.

I improvised a verse and recited it to drumbeat, Cab Calloway style.

> *Pretty little flower petals falling down*
> *don't look so fresh when you're out on the town.*
>
> *There's a certain kind of chit that be calling "hello,"*
> *out on the Garden Bridge stopping every fellow*
>
> *She hollers, "Soap is a* fen *and the towel is free.*
> *I'm xiaojie, daddy, now who wants me?"*

A fen was about a nickel. *Xiaojie* was Chinese for "young lady," but also slang for a whore. I had borrowed a bit from Memphis Minnie's "Dirty Dozen." Somehow I think she'd approve.

When Lotus Petal opened her mouth to object, I signaled the music to start. The drummer rippled his snare and pedaled the bass. Père counted down to a racy version of "Love for Sale" and the audience roared with laughter. Lotus Petal turned on her bound feet and minced her way to the door.

Père told me I'd been too hard on her. "Who are you to be throwing stones? Y'all both a couple of good-time gals keeping the enemy warm at night."

"You're just mad he's Japanese. That man's been nothing but good to me. What do you expect me to do? Leave him?"

"You can lead him down the garden path, for all I care. Tie him to a tree and leave him for tiger feed. We got bombs dropping around us and y'all fighting over a no-count man."

"But she barged in here trying to show me out in front of my audience."

"*En fait,* it's *my* audience, " he objected. "Last time I checked Père Prettiman and his Manhattan Revue was the name up there on the marquee."

"*Featuring* Luz Acosta Lee, the Harlem Nightingale, don't forget. Whose side are you on anyway? That chit tried to make me lose face."

In China, losing face was the ultimate act of public disgrace. But mine wasn't the one sacrificed. Lotus Petal's mug was left on the dance floor that night to be flattened beneath the Black Bottom stomp and jitterbugging feet.

I'd grown up in Matanzas, Cuba among people trading cheerful insults down at the docks. I was too shy and faltering to join in the game. After all, I was the child whose nickname was *Malabla* for "mala habla," mangled speech.

One day as my father sat mending fishing nets, a passerby laughed at his war wounds.

"*Oye, pantalón vacio.*" He'd called him "Empty-pants-leg."

Papí smiled and gave a friendly wave. Then he proceeded to call into question the man's entire pedigree. Witches, goats, cockroaches, cane rats, and women of ill repute were mentioned.

My father ended the exchange by telling the man to go ask his wife. "She'll tell you if my trouser leg is empty or not."

I could tell the man was livid but he didn't let it show. How would it look stooping down to fight a one-legged man? Getting angry in a war of words only showed you up as the loser.

Years later I heard the dozens played in Chicago streets and nightclubs. No one with any sense dared heckle a blues musician. Why, they'd stop in the middle of a song and roast you like a goose. Memphis Minnie was known for it. She'd disgrace somebody's mama in a "lordy-lord."

Iron is iron and steel won't rust
Your mama got a pussy like a Greyhound bus

Memphis Minnie wasn't from Memphis, and her name wasn't Minnie, either. Most people wouldn't dream of calling her into account. Would you want to get dirty-dozened by the likes of Lizzie Douglas from Tunica County, Mississippi?

I should think not.

Inheritance

Aparna Rajan

He hid under the cot, lying in wait.

The last time he had used the stakeout—it hadn't been a stakeout then, more like a hiding place—was when he had hidden from his Achamma to escape taking a bath. He hated baths. The only place Achamma would never enter in the house was Achan's room. It was out of bounds. He knew she would stop at the threshold, peep inside, and leave reluctantly, murmuring to herself, hoping she would find him elsewhere. Served her right, he had thought. It was a long time ago, more than six years, surely? He had been a boy then. Now, he was in the clumsy in-betweenness with his cracking—more like croaking—voice. No longer a boy, not yet a man.

The last time he'd hidden under the cot, he had barely registered what happened in the room. Both of them had been angry—the woman had used words he hadn't understood then. However, he had vivid memories of the whispered threats. "Don't you dare tell this to anyone." His Achan's contorted face. All he wanted was to leave the room and run to his mother. She had gone away to her home to attend a cousin's wedding. He had made a mental note to make her promise never to leave him behind again. Later, when he had been wandering at the back of the house, munching a ripe tamarind, trying to decide whether to meet Sam or watch TV, he had seen Achamma and the woman talking—in hurried whispers, again. Why did everyone except Achan whisper in this house? He had not had the patience to watch them go on and on and had rushed to Sam's house to play with him, though the image of the two of them murmuring in the backyard—Achamma, sad and resigned, almost pleading, and the woman angry and red—was etched in his memory.

Amma was away, again. This time, it was for three days. He didn't care as much as before. They didn't speak a lot these days. Not since he sprouted thin black shadows scrawled above his upper lip and in other places on the body. That's what he thought he saw when he checked himself out in the mirror. A scrawny shadow. He barely shared daily banter with Amma about school and cricket. He had grudgingly slid out of his daily reveries and hooked his eyes on his textbook pages when he heard her footsteps outside his room. The only time he felt an oddly comforting warmth was when they exchanged knowing glances over dinner whenever Achan bickered curses at her. Amma's glance pleaded, "Please leave it, I'm fine." The boy's silence hung ashamedly over the dinner table.

Amma always defended Achan. Maybe she was right. He did have a lot of things on his plate, and though he would occasionally get angry at them all, he liked Achan more than he let on. Achan was more handsome than Sam's father. Achan did not play with him like Sam's father, but everyone noticed when Achan entered a room. Something in his gaze turned people quiet. He always liked it when Achan came for his school meetings instead of Amma.

It felt like he had inherited a special charm. Just like his father, they all said. The way he crossed his feet, dangling one over the other, as he sat on bus stop benches with Achan, waiting to pick up Amma. The way he pressed his right palm on his stomach exactly two seconds before letting out a long burp. The way strands of his hair, on the right side of the middle parting stood upright, not giving in to the curls like the rest of his hair.

"It's like Kuttan came out of a Xerox copying machine," the aunty next door bellowed. She always called him Kuttan, which he usually hated but was willing to overlook on this particular occasion. He wondered why he was beaming with a vague pride as he remembered her words.

Achan never spoke much. He didn't have to. His presence commanded a silence that was respectful… almost fearful. It felt nice, to think that someday, he too might be able to turn an entire room silent just by walking into it. It was magic, how his father didn't need a lot of words to communicate. A glance, a twitch, a growl. When he did speak… to be honest, he preferred Achan's silence to his thunderous bellow.

His thoughts were interrupted when a familiar smell entered his nostrils. The stale saline stench of sweat mixed with the sweetish scent of *paan*. Achan was talking to someone. Two pairs of feet entered the room. Achan turned and bolted the door.

The boy adjusted his position and pressed himself further onto the side of the wall. A gossamer web dangled down from the edges of the wall, brushing his temples. He had seen her only once, though he knew her name. No—not her, this was another woman. Younger, more beautiful. It was last month, at the wedding of a relative, that he'd caught a glimpse of her while running down the stairs with his friends. The sight of red bangles dangling loose over her pale, dusky arms triggered something unnameable within him. Something flashed through his body. A jolt in his underbelly. A wave of a strange emotion washed over him. And all this, in a millisecond. Or was it more? It was hard to keep track of time. It was hard to notice his surroundings at that moment.

Desire brewed inside him. It was as if his body flared up. He could feel every inch of it, the contours, the curves, the crevices. He was suddenly aware that he possessed a body. A body that had begun acting crazy, behaving quite strangely. He had excused himself from his friends and sat under the banyan tree near the temple for a while, to calm his senses.

And it was this jolt that had led to the current uncomfortable scenario he was in. He readjusted his position so that he could stretch his legs. They had begun to ache. Ashes from last night's mosquito-repellent coil scattered over his pants. He still couldn't describe what exactly had happened. When he overheard the name of the woman, that she'd be coming over today to meet Achamma as she was passing by the area, he couldn't help himself. He had to see, he had to know. He was sure that she was coming over to meet Achan. He just knew. With Amma being away, it all seemed to fit in. He sometimes liked making up scenarios in his head—how, when he grew up, he would charm women like his Achan and how they would travel kilometers just to meet him and … and… He blushed at the thought.

He had been reading when she arrived. As suspected, she did not talk much to Achamma. She had already eaten, she said politely. Achan had come out of his room to greet her, and it was then, when he was sure no one would miss him, that he had rushed inside Achan's room and hid himself. It hadn't been as easy as before. He had lost track of how much he had grown in the past months. He had to tuck in his belly and squeeze himself under the cot.

He strained his neck to look up from under the bed. She was standing behind Achan, checking out the calendar on the wall. If only he could have a better view. And then she started speaking. Her voice was sweet, sweeter than Amma's. It had a slow calculated jingle to it, as if she spoke in musical notations. He liked it. Surprisingly, Achan spoke in hushed tones. He didn't think Achan would know how to. He could make out some of the words. He could hear Amma's name whispered more than once.

She must have said something that annoyed Achan, for he abruptly forgot to whisper. He turned away from him, towards her. He could see the muscles on the back of his father's neck tighten. He prayed that the woman dropped the subject, whatever it was. Make him less angry. The vein behind Achan's neck twitched. *Please find the right words, like Amma manages to,* he prayed to himself through gritted teeth. There was no way this woman could discern how feral Achan could get.

There was a sudden shuffle of feet. Though he couldn't see clearly, he could feel the movements in the room. Achan moved closer to the woman. He tried to hold her hand in the same instant that she tried to turn away from him. There was an overlap of grunts and a broken piece of glass bangle fell to the floor. The red shard of glass triggered something within him. He closed his eyes.

Desire and shame sprouted wings together. Twin feelings, born together, in the same instant. Each pushed the other to the sidelines, battling to take precedence. Both failed together. Neither took flight. Neither resigned to defeat. He was pulled into the battle, though reluctantly. He wanted to scream "stop" and run out of the room into the comfort of oblivion.

The night seemed to drone on, unhurriedly. Nothing around him seemed to realise the urgency of the situation. The cobwebs dangled dangerously close to his nose. He half-wished that they caused a loud sneeze; at least, everything would just end. He would be free. But nothing of the sort happened. The nightmare continued.

Why was he in the room? What had he wanted? All he could remember was a vague feeling of excitement that had jolted his spine. But this was nothing like he imagined. It was so far from it that he felt guilty. He knew he was betraying Amma somehow, though he didn't know how or why.

He was mad at himself for planning any of this. What was he even thinking? He wasn't a child anymore. How could he have gotten himself into such a fix? Maybe enduring this was the punishment he needed. He felt vaguely comforted by that thought. He wished Achamma would knock on the door, looking for him. But he knew it was the last place she would look for.

When he opened his eyes, after what seemed like hours, the *pallu* of her saree had slithered down on the floor. In the dim light reflecting off the dingy room, it seemed to move stealthily towards him, like an uncoiling snake making a hasty getaway. He felt a pang in his heart. Amma had a similar colour saree, but of a different material. He had often helped her hold the pleats while she draped the saree hurriedly as she rushed for work every morning. Why did he keep thinking about Amma? He blinked away the hot tears forming in his eyes.

They were speaking now, Achan's voice getting louder. He heard a sob in between. He was surprised. Did that mean… did that mean… she didn't want to be there? Did she feel trapped, just like him? He had imagined differently, and now he couldn't be more wrong. But then, she was the one who had come to their house… well, he too had hidden himself in the room willingly. And now, there was nothing he wouldn't give, just to get out of the room. As the realisation dawned on him, he felt his body shiver.

He felt stuck in the dusty space under the cot like never before. An awkward in-between. It was worse than existing as a shadow. For the first time in his life, he didn't want to grow out of it. He didn't want to be like Achan. Or like anyone. He was content, being a shadow. All he wanted was to erase every shred of memory of this day from his brain. He thought about Amma… and a sob escaped his throat. It slowly turned into a wail, emerging from the depths of his body. But by then, he no longer cared if he was heard.

Mother Tongue

Jocelyn A. Chin

When you speak, they call it broken. A sentence snapped, its meaning jerked back. An open wound in the grammar, a limp in the syntax. Vocabulary scattered in pieces. Every act of translation is an act of violence.

I'm not sure when I learned to be cautious, to avoid the pain of being on an island of short syllables and strange tones. There used to be a pride in me, a trust in our language, from a time too deep for me to withdraw a memory from. Decades ago, when you picked me up from my first day of preschool, my teacher jokingly remarked, "I learned how to say 'green frog' in Mandarin today!" She had continuously pointed to a picture of a frog, with the words "green frog" below it, reading the words to me. Every time I would reply, "qīng wā." "Green frog," she returned with another point. "Qīng wā," I insisted. *Green frog.* Point. *"Qīng wā."* I never gave in, and eventually my teacher decided that I would teach her new vocabulary instead. You laugh at my stubbornness whenever you share this story, and I always cringe in mild embarrassment.

Growing up, Grandma told me a story about a sparrow who sang too loudly, and a mean old woman cut off its tongue. I think Grandma's version is a Japanese folktale that had somehow wound its way to Taiwan, a story in which a sparrow had eaten grains that the old woman had been saving, and in her fury she cut off its tongue then chased it away. But luckily for sparrow-lovers, it was a magical bird, so its tongue grew back.

Grandma always had many cautionary tales, though I find their lessons unclear. In Anderson's book of fairytales, a Chinese emperor banished his nightingale friend after receiving a bejeweled automaton bird that sang to him instead – but as the years flowed, its cogs wore down. When the emperor was lying on his deathbed, his old nightingale friend returned to the kingdom to sing to him, and its beautiful song restored his health.

The summer we visited Yellowstone, I ran around the RV camp, laughing in the sunshine, but Grandma pulled me over by the forearm and whispered in my ear that wicked folks lurked in parks to steal little girls from their families, and these evil men would stuff a cloth in your mouth so you couldn't call for help. I was scared to step out of your sight for days.

You always told me not to take Grandma's words too seriously, whether it was about birds or the murders of little girls. You winked at me when she wasn't watching. You told me to keep running, to keep laughing out loud. You told me I'm safe and swaddled me in hand-crocheted scarves and storybooks about moons and rabbits and love.

In the story of the tongue-cut sparrow, there was also a kind old man. He had loved the sparrow and when he learned what the old woman had done, he searched and searched throughout the forest. He eventually found the sparrow and its family, and they rewarded the old man for his dedication and kindness with a basket of jewels.

For a while, I thought there were happy endings if you are willing to become a bird. In a Greek tragedy, Philomena's brother-in-law rapes her and cuts off her tongue, but she transforms, vengefully, into a nightingale, and is able to sing her lament forever. I imagined her new tongue setting forest upon forest ablaze with sorrow. But I just learned recently that female nightingales are actually mute, and only the males in the species sing.

You remember when you first began dreaming in English after moving to the U.S. from Taiwan. A friend once told me she became fluent in French when she began dreaming in French after her study-abroad. It's easy to think of these dreams as some sort of milestone, a barrier crossed from passing traveler to fluent speaker, no longer a sojourner but at home in a language in your dreams at last. But a few months after we moved to China from Chicago, when I forgot the English words for "alligator" and "sunflower" in a dream, I woke up with green reptiles and golden petals on my mind, frustration and fear brewing in my chest. I called it a nightmare, and I was furious. I wanted to remember the names of things. English was my familiar, subconscious, linguistic home, and Mandarin was swooping into my dreamscape, stealing it away.

I'm still learning the depths of your thoughts within the constraints of translation from your mind to your mouth to my ears to my mind. To those who do not pay attention – how are you not withering in guilt? *Jiā yóu* becomes just *good luck* and *xīn kǔ* becomes merely *hard work*. I once ran past a xiaolongbao place named *lù míng chūn* – it means *when the sound of a fawn tells you of the arrival of spring*. Whoever translated it to English called it "Joe's Shanghai." The difference between two names is the cultural rift immigrants must daily cross.

I'm trying to learn to hear you speak so that you do not have to control your tongue. Let your broken sentences flow.

Because one day, the new tongue moves so painlessly that you do it without thinking, like swallowing. Because to open our mouths really is to do the simplest thing. We enter the world wailing, and along the way, someone tells a story to turn our cries into song.

Of Those Who Lived and Died

Poetry Collection

Cathy Millangue

Cathy Millangue

Rizal's Flowers

You can wrap your hands around me
and squeeze
and say you are just holding me,
like how God wraps His hands around His children.
But if so,
why are the bodies of my priestesses
and those that challenge your binary view
buried underneath my dirt?
How can you call me ignorant
when you yourself do not wish to learn?

You can prune dissidents,
"weeds,"
that dare to break above the ground
and raise their heads towards the sun.
But even if you do,
you will never remove the roots
woven into the Earth.

You can save me,
"liberate" me,
"free" me,
but when I decide
that I will no longer bow,
you deem me
too uncivilized
to govern myself,
that I need you
to teach me scripture (even though that already happened),
to make me moral.

More like you.
But is it not myself
that knows myself the most?
My needs? My limits? My strengths?

You can sit in my home
and act like it is your right to be there,
that I must serve you the flesh of my own.
You believe
that my garden
is yours for the taking
and bleed me dry.
When you are done,
you leave the scars of war
on my men,
women,
and children
and pretend
that they are not wrapped
in bandages,
that they are completely healed.

As much as you--or anybody--
tries
to bury the truth,
bury me,
you will never succeed.

Cathy Millangue

There will always be flowers
that fight to grow in the sun,
knowing that so many
have fought and died
to see them do so.

And no matter how far
my seeds have been strewn
or how scared, how vulnerable, how hopeless they've become
they will always find a way
to plant their roots
and reach towards a clear sky
and feel the warmth of sunlight.

Aquino's Tale

Let's set the scene
      of a story told to me
            When I was older (but not really):
I guess I have to add context:
the Pacific Front of World War II
my great-grandfather (Isabelo) was in it.
I suppose the rest of his family was, too
but they were back at home
elders, women, and children.

My great-grandmother (Leonore)
took care of their daughters
and spent her life
stooped over her land
planting rice
and caring for her mother and father.

And one day, Leonore was in the field,
children and parents at home,
her husband away as corporal
                            guerilla,
                                 and shield.

On that day, the sun wasn't alone in the sky:
strange sounds, strange clouds
the scream of sirens,
forecast of nails raining from the sky.

She
                    ran
                                     back,
across the fields
along with others trying to scramble away from the attack.

Leonore knew she was her family's shield
while Isabelo was gone.
She would not let her children feel
like they were only
bullet points
--steps--
that they were sacrificial pawns.
She would not die without seeing her parents,
the ones who first protected her
in a world that eats its children.

And luckily
the metal rain hit only trees
and not her family.

Thank God,

Isabelo could yet see
with his own eyes
his second-born
for the first time.

That is
if he had lived.

The Spaces Inside

Karina Cheah

Last year, instead of joining my family in Penang, Malaysia for Chinese New Year, I FaceTimed my parents after everyone returned together from the reunion meal. I wanted the screen to be a curtain I could step through from my living room in Norwich, England to join everyone in my parents' Airbnb, surrounded by the chatter of my aunties and uncles, picking at the snacks on the dining table despite being over-full from the meal. This year, although it is two weeks before the New Year, all four of us are in Penang: my parents, my sister, and I.

My aunties, uncle, cousin, grandma, and my great-aunt would pile into our Airbnb's living room after a steamboat lunch. Granny was craving steamboat, and she's grown fussy about her food, so when she's set on something, we go. The collaborative, cook-as-you-eat nature of steamboat is how I'd imagined reunion lunch: utensils and intentions colliding as we added seafood, meatballs, vegetables, and noodles from apparently bottomless plates to the bubbling pot of soup in the center of our table.

Even though we staggered through the last few plates at lunch, my mother now sets a bowl of peeled, shredded pomelo and a handful of forks on the dining table. My Auntie BC emerges from the kitchen with a plate of precisely cut rectangles of layer cake and opens the jars of snacks—peanutty crisps, buttery love letters, flaky pineapple tarts. Next to her, my Uncle Jonathan deals the hands for a card game, and my Auntie Cally explains the rules to my sister and parents while my great-aunt and my grandma settle onto the couch. I make a cup of tea, take it to the coffee table, and sit on the floor, my Auntie Sharon across from me and Auntie BC to my right.

I want to ask what I often wonder when we gather: "Do you wish we saw each other more?" and "Do you resent my dad for moving so far away from this island" — where he grew up around the people in this room, to the east coast of the United States of America?

"Dear Silence," writes Victoria Chang, "[…] *What are you doing? What's at stake here?* […] *Why are you circling around and around, afraid to go into the center?* I think I am circling around you, Silence, your center, and the closer I get, the closer I am to shame, to the language of shame."[1]

I circle around the unfamiliar shapes of Hokkien I'd never learned because we communicate exclusively in English: the everlasting legacy of the British Empire. I circle around my American accent that three years of living in England failed to erase; and around this island of my dad's youth that I only know in patchwork, which I have only visited twice in the past five years. I ache to spend more time here, the kind of soft pain that carves through me so insidiously that I don't notice it until the plane lands and I see PENANG INTERNATIONAL AIRPORT in block letters through the tiny window, and I step out into warm humidity and high-rises and hawker centers, and the island floods the spaces inside me.

The questions brim at my lips, fresh with readiness, but I will say nothing. I will eat another pineapple tart when Granny offers me the rest of her plate of snacks.

It is easy to fill the silences that exist in this room. The shouting from the card game at the dining table, because my sister keeps winning. The conversation between me and Auntie Sharon about the movies we saw this year, and how much we cried at *The Wild Robot*. The soft smile on Granny's face, though she appears to be taking a nap, and the chuckle from my great-aunt, as they eavesdrop on the card game behind them. The soft clatter of forks against plates and plates against tables as we deplete the snacks.

"Maybe silence is not something to interact with, to be filled in," Chang writes, "but rather to let wash over you, to exist within. […] Maybe silence is also a life lived. […] Maybe it's the most open text. The loudest form of speaking we have." [2]

Maybe the questions in the back of my throat do not matter in the way that I think they do. Does someone need to affirm the wish to see one another more, for it to be true? How much does it matter that my dad left Penang for a life in America when, during each visit, laughter spills from around our lunch table, overflows into the apartment, and leaves its traces in the air? When this island, no matter how many years elapse between visits, folds me into its embrace and fills me to the brim with dim sum and chrysanthemum tea and the love we do not speak?

I hug my Auntie BC, and she rests her head on my shoulder. My cousin perches on the arm of the couch next to my great-aunt, his grandmother, and joins the conversation. He is looking forward to starting art college in a few days' time. When the card game ends, Uncle Jonathan and Auntie Cally meander over, picking up the thread of a conversation about their trip to Japan that we left at the steamboat table.

Later, we will take family photos with Uncle Jonathan's phone and tripod, as we have each time my family visits. My great-aunt will press red envelopes with ringgit notes into the hands of me and my sister, even though it is not yet New Year, and I will hold mine close to my chest, trying to fit my family inside.

[1] Victoria Chang, Dear Memory: Letters on Writing, Silence, and Grief (Milkweed Editions, 2021), 12.

[2] Chang, Dear Memory, 145.

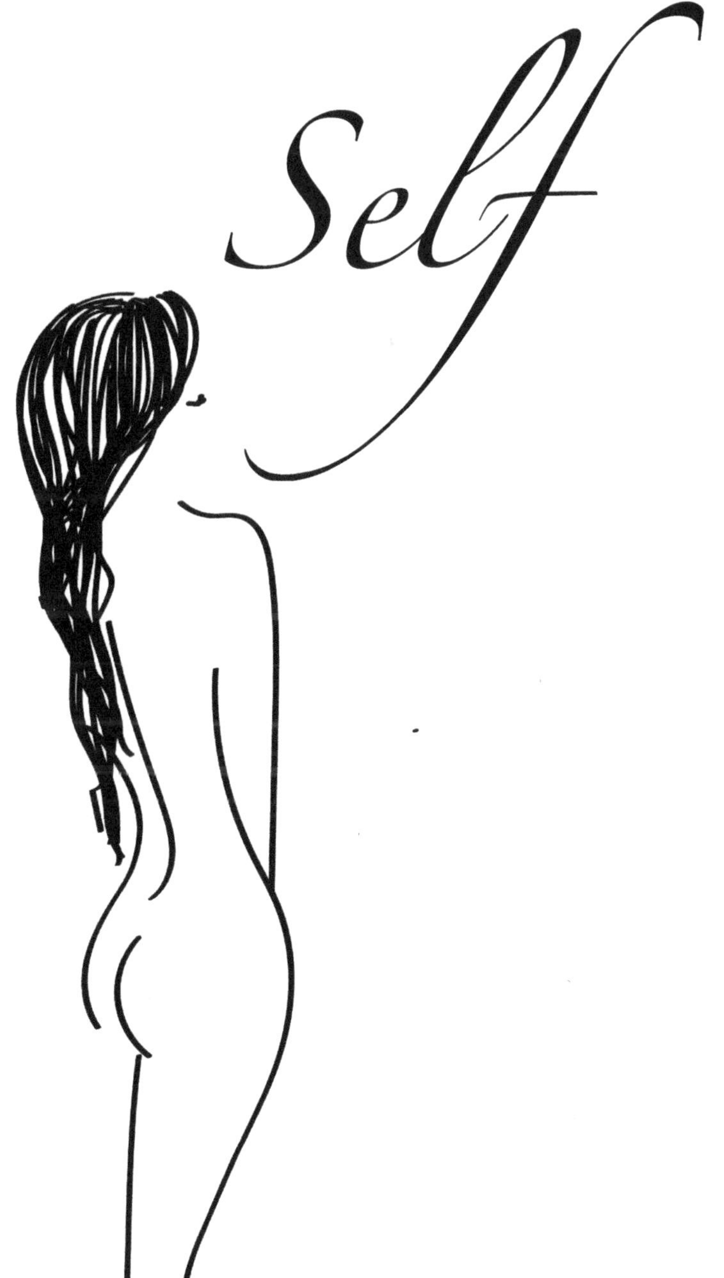
Self

my name is Farah

Farah Art Griffin

Farah Art Griffin

my name is Farah

the
name
Parah
is not mine
tag disfigurement
intolerance into deep sea
as the moniker beckons me, my voice cannot swim
it ripples to my brain, "utter something, why aren't you speaking,
say my name is Farah"

lucky girl

Poetry Collection

Tara Lall

lucky girl

i don't think i'm ugly
but i do think that i make others feel lucky
lucky that they have smooth, kind edges
lucky that they carry their weight in other places
lucky that their hands are delicate
lucky that god chose me and not them.

i make up for it, i think, in the way i move
and the way the darkness covers my resting
face—i relate a lot to the moon in that way
i'd like to make up for it in song, as well
ideally, i wouldn't have to make up for it at
all. alas, we live in a society.

fragmentation

there are marks on my veins
they dance around my pores
duck under the cysts
and bleed over the bones
outlining my skeleton for those who care enough to look.

my words are mixed in salt
tossed in caramelised onions
seared in sauce and spilled
over and over again—
fusion cuisine, they call it.

i cannot communicate with you
i cannot get you under
my skin, past my bones, through my faults
you just don't fit—
perhaps, that's why my head lies against yours now.

as it happens, before
i lay my head—
a familiar action
once repeated between father and daughter
now onto daughters
for we find strength in numbers.

Actor Network Theory

I am not an actor, but I know how to make you miss it.

The silence.

The absence, the negative space, one less plate to clean and one less mouth to feed.

I make sure your shower is on before turning mine up,
I make sure that all the socks I choose to wear
slide easily on these floors,
and I know where every light can be seen from.

I know that door likes to creak when you open past the mark on the floor,
I know that sofa has a spot that
sinks more than the rest, I know that table has 3 marks so
they must always be covered by my hand every
breakfast without fail on repeat or I risk losing my place to stay.

I know the exact force I need to turn on the lights
without making that *click* sound that you hate, I know
how to flip a page so quietly you will not notice, I know
how to eat my food with such quiet bites, even the
food doesn't realise half of it is gone until it's too late.

I know how to listen for your steps,
the frequency at which I should expect
a negative reaction from their arrival,
and just how long that arrival will take.

I know that I am in debt and you are an investor,

but no one sees their investments grow up, do they?

Is that why you're not here anymore?

I am not an actor, but I know how to act
like I'm not around, thanks to you.
I am not an actor, but when you were not around
I loved to act as if nobody was around.
I am not an actor… but I was.

Light

with your blood, caressing

the inside of my bones

the gold, blessing

the mould, just fitting

around my legs

the flames snake up and take

my legs, stuck.

my legs… are stuck.

i am licked through the scrappy meat we call skin

and yet i feel no pain

for what was once a malnourished,

mistreated, untouched and unloved

piece of a thirteen-year-old

turns into a puddle of gold.

they must not have learned their lesson

nor noticed a missing son

because my eyes can't seem to focus on theirs as i hear 'light it up.'

G

I own a guitar, yes
I contributed no penny in buying it.
In reality, my hands were meant to borrow
And never to own

Until one Christmas,
I received it as a gift.
It wasn't wrapped under the tree,
And no eyes expectantly watched for
A twitch on my cheek
A smile hiding under my laughter.

I received it after coming home from the hospital.
The guitar wasn't the only thing I received,
But oh how I wished it had been.

It's a beautiful guitar.
The tawny amber shines so bright.
I can not only see my reflection, but the faces before me.
The fretboard has marks where my father used to carefully
Place his calloused fingers as gently as he did
When he placed his fingers on my head to give me a kiss
Those marks still remain and I thank them for their presence
Or rather, their absence.

My father's favourite chord was G.

To me, it was always a misshapen triangle;

To him, it could tell stories.

The first chord I played on that guitar was

G

Toxic

Linh Truong

My husband doesn't know that he's in love with me. I suspect he believes he's doing a fine job of pretending to be in love with me, but if he'd wanted a doltish wife, he wouldn't have chosen one from Shānxīn Island.

The servants announce my arrival at his chambers with nothing more than a subdued knock. He is expecting me, as he has every fortnight since our marriage nine moons ago. He doesn't open his eyes when I enter, and I don't bow.

"Wench," he greets me.

"My lord," I simper in reply. There's no audience for us to perform for, but I know how much my obsequiousness rankles him, so I persist even in the privacy of his chambers. He doesn't halt his meditation to meet my gaze but, sure enough, his annoyance seeps into my skin as if he had.

I make my way further into the room towards the low table where the components for our evening tea have already been set out. I've long been accustomed to preparing tea, so I watch my husband as my hands go through the motions. He doesn't look as peaceful as one should when meditating; his years of scowling have already etched themselves into his skin despite his youth. Derisive as the set of his brows may be, they can do little to mar the natural beauty he possesses.

He is a savage sort of beautiful, different from the sort of savage that I am, but no less dangerous. His hair is as long and as dark as mine, left loose now that he's retired to his chambers for the night. Where my skin is lightly bronzed from a childhood spent in the sun, his is a fair, flawless porcelain that can only be achieved through a lifetime of privilege. His phoenix eyes are bladed and harsh, his regal nose and sculpted cheekbones belie his birth. His brushstroke mouth is lovely only in sleep, without his waking scowl to impair it. He looks angry, always, and I wish I were not too prideful to admit to enjoying his rare moments of mirth. But I am prideful, made even more so when I notice that the neck of his evening robes has loosened in the time since he changed into them, exposing the only permanent scar he has; a thin, curved line just below his collarbone. I don't comment on his choice to expose the mark I'd cleaved onto him the night of our wedding, nor the color of his attire. Blue. I've always loved him in blue.

I'm wearing blue as well, as I've always loved myself in blue.

I don't know how he thinks he's fooling anyone but himself. With how meticulous he is, there's no way that none of this was intentional. Perhaps, if pressed, he'll claim that he only means to lessen the strain on my delicate eyes by dressing in colors resembling the dusky evening rather than his courtly reds and golds. Perhaps he's not displaying his scar and was simply too absorbed in his meditation while awaiting his beloved wife to adjust his robes when they loosened. The dusting of red high on his cheekbones can be attributed to the heat coming from the numerous candles and lanterns littering the antechamber, or so he would have me believe. I humor him, as I have for the past two moons.

I finish preparing the tea and pour us each a small cup. After a quick glance to make sure his eyes are still closed, I pull a small vial out of the inner pocket in my sleeve. With hands made silent from years of practice, I unstopper the vial and pour its contents into the cup that's meant to be his.

While there's no discernible odor, the liquid is a profuse green, dyeing the tea a mossy peat color that is quite a ways off from the clear amber of Háorui's favorite white-tip oolong. Out of the folds of my sash, I pull out another vial, which I pour into my own cup. The pandan extract isn't quite as ruddy, but it turns my tea into a close approximation of the shade my husband's is.

I have little confidence that this will be enough to kill him, but I hope that it will significantly inconvenience him.

I set his cup across from mine at the low table and put away the implements I used to make the tea, clanking slightly more than necessary to alert him that I've finished. I hear no noise from his corner of the room, but the hairs at my nape stand on end with the weight of his stare.

"Part of the appeal of tea is the fact that it's hot, you know," I say. I know it irks him when I don't look at him while speaking, so I busy myself with tidying the tea tray and allow myself a smirk at his agitated huff. There's a rustle of fabric and a muted *crack* from what must be his neck as he straightens. I see the skirt of his robes first, then a glimpse of his bare calves, then he is before me as he lowers himself to his knees with the faltering inelegance of someone unused to kneeling. I like the look of it on him.

Háoruì casts a discerning look towards the tea, no doubt noting the peculiar color, but nonetheless accepts the cup with a bow that is gracious only because everything else has been beaten out of him.

"My thanks, honored wife," he says with all the liveliness of an expired toad. For all his carefully constructed civility, though, he slams the drink into his mouth as if it were a draught of rice wine. There is space for one breath, then he leans over, heaving and coughing, braced with one hand to the floor and the other over his mouth.

"What did—" he manages to gasp out before succumbing again. I expected this reaction, planned for it, but the sight of him weakened and convulsing sends my pulse rocketing. A linen kerchief had been ready in my hand since he reached for the cup, and I offer it to him without a word, not wanting to risk him hacking up blood onto the beautiful silk embroidery of his sleeve. His eyes are furious at me, but he swipes the cloth from my hand and holds it to his face as he continues to retch.

A few seconds pass, and I note that his eyes have begun to water and the skin of his neck has turned sallow and wan. I take in slow breaths through my nose and hope the coloration isn't permanent, as I am rather fond of his neck. A few seconds more and his coughs have turned into gasps as the arm supporting him trembles violently before giving out.

I rise and make my way around the table to settle near his head and observe. I don't clench my hands together. No, I place them very purposefully on my knees and breathe through my nose and ignore my heartbeat pounding in my throat. He's been convulsing for nearly three minutes. Quite a long time, considering the strength of the poisons I had given him. Still, it's longer than I expected.

"Do you want the antidote?" I know my face is perfectly blank and my voice perfectly even, but the fact that I have to ask betrays my concern.

One would think that after doing this once every fortnight for the better part of a year, I would be used to seeing my husband in pain.

Háoruì writhes and wheezes still, but his eyes are fierce and unclouded as they meet mine.

"I'm not," he growls, "bleeding yet."

And he's not. The kerchief is dirtied only by spittle and a faint smear of green when he lets it fall from his grip. He's still shuddering, wracked with a faltering cough, even as his eyes stay glued to mine. The hand that relinquished the kerchief clenches and unclenches around nothing. I ignore that my heart does the same at first, but I can't ignore the urge to brush away the hair that's fallen over his face. A moment of weakness, which soon stretches into another as I slip my hand into his.

Hours or minutes or seconds pass as we wait out the poison together, his hand a desperate vice around mine. But eventually, the tremors subside and he breathes heavily but unhindered. Only then does he press his eyes closed and loosen his grip on my hand. I pull away slowly, intending to return my hands to my lap but succumb to the desire to smooth his hair away once more.

I trail my fingers through his locks and carefully pick out the tangles he accrued during his fit. I'm arranging them to fall smoothly behind his neck, a curtain of ink spilled against pristine parchment, when, very lightly, he rests his fingertips against my ankle.

I'm hesitant to speak, to interrupt the fragile softness he's shown me, but he's been lying on the floor for nearly half an hour and I know he'll be even more surly if I allow him to wallow any longer.

I trace the shell of his ear with my fingers, so delicate and soft compared to the hardness of his other features, and feel his breath catch when I smooth my hand down his cheek. He's very foolish, I think, to fall in love with the person whose sole purpose in the kingdom of Tiānxià is to poison him. I am equally foolish.

"Háoruì," I murmur, using his given name, which he allows me only during these rare moments of vulnerability. I feel him stiffen in degrees as he rebuilds his armor. I make to rise, intending to give him a moment to himself, but his hand at my ankle stills me. I pause, but he releases my ankle without a word and goes to leverage himself into a sitting position.

I don't offer to aid him, knowing that any sympathy would only chafe at him right now. Instead, I go back to my side of the table and make him a fresh cup of tea. By the time he joins me, I can see no traces of his previous distress save for a slight redness around his eyes. He is my lord once again, my husband tucked away where he thinks he can't be hurt.

He takes the cup I offer without comment and downs it similarly to the first, does the same for the third and fourth, and finally on the fifth allows himself a pause. "What the hell was in that?" His voice is tightly controlled, though I know he must be seething.

I fight back a shrug and keep my gaze forward and my tone perfunctory as I list the ingredients in the cocktail of poisons. I don't explain what each does, as he is almost as familiar with them as I am.

"Oh, and parsley root," I finish. His face goes through a myriad of emotions before settling on disgust, which I take to mean he's fully recovered. My shoulders, tense after all this time, tremble slightly in my effort to hold back a laugh.

"*Parsley root*," he parrots back incredulously. He hates parsley.

"For the flavor," I offer, allowing myself a shrug this time. He sputters quite unbecomingly for a royal and tension eases out of me in the form of a giggle. "I *hate* parsley." The giggle has turned into a full guffaw and I can see him now. My husband, peeking through the veil of propriety. He sets a scowl on his face and finally meets my eyes. "By the gods, woman, are you trying to kill me?!"

"That's the idea," I say as innocently as I can manage. The crinkle of his nose and his sideways look lets me know he isn't amused by my cheekiness.

"Well, that might be the closest you've come so far," he mutters. Dragging a hand down his face, I can just barely make out an exasperated, "*Parsley root.*"

He knocks back his sixth cup of tea with a vehemence that can only be fueled by spite. I watch the line of his throat as he swallows, letting my

gaze drift down to the gaping neck of his robes, loose enough now that I can just see the dip of his navel. It's well past indecent, and the relief in my stomach warms, settling as a low, simmering heat that urges me to take him to bed. His body has none of the chiseled strength possessed by the warriors I so admired as a girl. Instead, Háoruì is smooth and polished, lithe from martial forms practiced under an undisturbed dawn rather than in combat.

I have enjoyed his body eagerly and often in the time since I forgave him the circumstances of our marriage, yet I still find myself transfixed by the planes of his chest. I set my desire aside, though, as we'd agreed that on nights like these, it would benefit his convalescence to avoid any strenuous activity. By the time my eyes return to his, there's color high on his cheeks and his breath halts sharply on the intake. I divert my gaze with an amused huff and set about peeling him a mandarin from the ever-present pile on the table.

I feed him as I go, stretching my arm across the table to offer the sections to him by hand. He refuses at first, ears flushed prettily at the tips and brows set firmly in their furrow, but acquiesces at my quirked brow. He's very, very bad at pretending.

"How was it?" I ask after he's eaten half a mandarin. He eats delicately, as stipulated by his royal upbringing, but quite at odds with his churlish countenance.

"Awful. Horrid. Repugnant." Only three adjectives this time, so it must not have been that bad, all things considered. As if sensing my rising humor, he adds, "I think I preferred the one that rendered me blind for a night."

He's looser, more relaxed now that the ordeal is over. I know he thinks he's been a dutiful husband to me since I put him in his place on our wedding night—and he has been—but I much prefer him this way. He's not as haughty or belligerent as he was before we married, not as stiff or cordial as he is when we're before the court. Here in the dark, after willingly putting his life in my hands, he is a wild, unrestrained thing. He forgets that he's pretending to love me. I don't remind him, because now I can see how he really loves me.

"Please," I say, snarking back at him. Routine as usual. "It wasn't anything you haven't had before." He glares at my dismissiveness, though it lacks heat because he knows I'm right. It was, altogether, not that strong a poison compared to the others I'd prepared for him before.

"It tasted like moldering cabbage steeped in goat manure." I can't hold back a snort at his description, making him glare even harder. "Like an odious pustule of aborted dreams and gangrene."

"You've been saving that one, haven't you?" I ask dryly. His scowl deepens, which means yes.

"You're supposed to be testing my tolerance for poison, not blasted parsley. Ten hells, I wanted to sear my tastebuds off. I ought to send you back to your putrid island of peasant-witches and demand a new poisons master."

"You'll find none finer than I, my lord," I demur mockingly. He scoffs but doesn't refute me.

The putrid island, as he put it, is home to the best herbalists in the kingdom. Accomplished scholars and herbalists from the mainland traveled often to the island just off the southern coast in hopes of apprenticing with my master. It was a highly coveted position, as she rarely took apprentices— only a handful every five years. Five years under the tutelage of my master was enough of a commendation to guarantee anyone the most prestigious of occupations, or the most foul.

My grandmother had hoped I would end up as a healer after she officially took me on as an apprentice when I was ten, and I suppose I could've managed that, as I am not unskilled in medicine. But it was clear very early on from my natural aptitude for poisons that I would be better suited as an assassin. By the time I finished my apprenticeship, only the leader of the Three Monkeys Mercenary Guild could rival my prowess. Four years after that, the Three Monkeys was leaderless and I had proven myself the finest poisons master on the continent.

A year after that, I was married to the only man who could not be poisoned. Though not for lack of trying, I muse, thinking back to the situation that unwittingly led to our marriage. He seemed so much younger then, despite it being less than a year ago. He'd come to the island after learning of my skill, determined to determine whether or not I was deserving of my reputation.

"You're sure that *this*," he'd gestured to where I was seething silently next to my grandmother in the sitting room of our manor on Shānxīn, "is the best? This girl has the knowledge to inoculate me from any poison that can be conceived?"

He addressed this to his advisor, who looked pityingly chastened at his lord's ire. My grandmother, wizened beyond any outward display of affront, placed a placating hand over mine where I fisted it in my robes.

"I can assure you, sire, that there has been none so accomplished as she since the time of His Excellence your grandfather," the adviser said, not looking at any of us. I kept my eyes trained on the young lord in defiance and wished my gaze was venomous enough that I might curdle the blood in his veins. He claimed to be immune to all poisons the royal herbalists could concoct, had been since he was a boy, and was determined to survive poisons even beyond what could be developed in the mainland. *We'll see about that*, I thought.

"She's a child," the young lord sniffed disdainfully. His eyes flicked to mine then quickly away, which I took as a small victory.

"Oh?" I sneered, heedless of the disrespect I had garnered by speaking out of turn. "And I suppose that makes you a juvenile."

He had no grounds to refer to me as a child when he knew full well that I was nearing the end of my second decade, and that I knew he was mere months past that age himself. His advisor, shocked at my outburst, came back to himself in a sputtering rush of half-formed rage. The flat of his palm met my cheek with surprising speed.

The advisor was old and not very strong, but his fingers were bony enough that I felt the impact on my tongue.

"Have him executed." My grandmother's voice, clear and imposing, rang in the silence that followed. She was looking directly at the young lord. There were no signs of fury on the aged lines of her face, only cold disdain. Perhaps that was what convinced him to incline his head in acquiescence, or perhaps there was something else in her eyes that I couldn't see from her profile.

"M-my lord," the advisor cried, clearly shocked that he would agree. "Please, sire, I only meant to teach the girl some respect. She is clearly unfit to be in your presence. The-the crone, as well! Who is she to demand such things? Sire, you must know I act only in your interests—the kingdom's interests!"

But the young lord was captive to my grandmother's stare. There was no haughty contempt on his youthful face now. Everyone knew that my grandmother was the most accomplished herbalist one could ever gain an audience with and that she would take disrespect from no one, not even the young lord. My grandmother extended a hand to me. It was not a gesture of comfort; she did not mean to take my hand as she had before. No, this was a command. Righting my clothes and adjusting my hair, I rose to my feet.

"A demonstration, then," my grandmother said. As an afterthought, she added, "if it should please Your Highness."

The advisor was groveling at the young lord's feet, begging for his life. It was clear the advisor was of no great importance to the young lord, as he inclined his head once more. I could feel that the rouge on my lips had smeared at the corner and I wiped it away with my thumb as I approached the sniveling advisor.

Finally, once I was before the young lord, he raised his eyes to mine.

"My lord," I said as obsequiously as I could manage. I didn't bow, nor did I kneel so that my head was below his. Instead, I stood above him as I held his eyes and wrenched the advisor's head back until his neck was craned toward the ceiling. Then I smeared my thumb, tinted red with rouge, against the advisor's mouth. He was dead within the minute.

The young lord's eyes were blown wide with fear or excitement or both, and I thought that he'd like to kiss me, to taste the poison directly from my lips.

"Zǐyún will be your wife and nothing less," my grandmother said, her voice ringing with finality. "No man, woman, child, or creature shall ever seek to injure her again. In return, she will ensure your health in the face of any poison known or imagined. Are we agreed?"

Two moons later, I tried to slit my newlywed husband's throat in our marriage bed. He was young and brash and foolhardy, and he'd done nothing to court my good graces. If he was so determined to greet death, I would be the one to introduce them. I had agreed that he would be safe from poison, and the blade was naked but for the glint of candlelight. He'd been rather more respectful after that.

The tight skin of his scar shines pale and uneven against the otherwise unblemished canvas of his chest. His hand begins to rise when he notices how my eyes have caught on it, to cover or frame the scar I'm not sure, but he aborts the motion with a jerk and lowers his hand back to the table. I raise my eyes to his and lick the mandarin juice from my fingers.

He can't seem to catch his breath, though I'm sure the effects of the poison have worn off by now. I wonder when, exactly, he fell in love with me, because the look in his eyes now is not dissimilar to the way he gazed at me after our first meeting. I wonder, too, when I fell in love with him, because sometime in the last few moons, I find that I'm glad none of my attempts on his life have proven successful.

Coup

Poetry Collection

Rishabh Motwani

Rishabh Motwani

Coup

Part 1: The Annexure

The mountain village off the grid,
bordering between passion and treason…
where we used to escape,
assume identities,
and roleplay,
rewind coded static radio messages,
because loving freely meant getting guillotined in this sovereign.

I assumed the farmer of the ranges,
waterlilies and lotus stems,
existing only for you—
we were both renegades.

You looked to the waters, and I to the pollination.
Who would ever suspect us here?

Each other's secret for more than a fortnight,
a century,
of days…
But when did it start getting old?
Did I lack substance?
Or the subtlety that gets hot but never bold?

I did it all—
the muse of all seasons,
the doer of all fields,
a bearer too, if I could.
But no, you pissed it all away.

Your rage, and its waves,
waterlogging all that should have stayed.

Uhh!!

I could do it again.
I would have—
in a heartbeat… in a second…

But…
You seceded,
ran after a redneck.
And I couldn't believe it—
a lover's squabble,
but I died a billion deaths.

Not our ponds of promised forever,
not these lotuses—
they're our children!

    Not you saying,
     "Your grandeurs of delusion bore no result.
     I am not yours to claim, never was.
     I am just a benefactor of good nature."
    You debaucherer!

I will show you love—
but what?
I'll burn, and it will only be warmer for you and your new charmer.

I won't fertilize the lands for you any longer.
So,
set the course. Blur the lines.
Move ahead with the annexure.
Declare me mad
as a march hare.

You have my head.

But you won't find me in that field, as promised,
beyond right and wrongdoings,
as Rumi said.
For you'd never shed your arrogance.

I'm faceless,
retribution none,
only grievance,
and existential crisis.

Who was I
if not yours, down to the last inch?

Part 2: Ex-Communicado

When did the idyllic mountains,
enveloped with perennial shower clouds,
morph into a scorching desert
with whiplashing embers and hell-whips?

Losing moisture,
as I lost my last links of association with you.

Panting,
like a newborn fowl desperate for its first ounce.

Lungs,
puffed so much,
they might burst…
if I mentioned you by name.

Half-living,
at the mercy of God
and his hell-web of all life,
that I detested to the point of sacrilege.

But I was in no position for assertion.

Dying my billionth death,
every second torment,
spilling my guts after the toil of the millionth wild tempest,
weaved from my poisoned imagination.
 "Grandeur of delusions," you said.

I screamed something foul in silence—
if my decibels could burst the sanctity of installed physics,
they would have.

My love—
a resource, dejected but all-powerful,
if only,
the wielder can harness it.

Ex-communicado.
Declared an outlaw,
a bounty on my head,
but I'm unrecognizable out of sorrow.
The only benediction of that ugly benefactor.

But when did my venomous lamentations
morph into ancient gospels?
Ask any of God's true servants—
helplessness breathed in me sermons.

Incanted or manifested,
a caregiver,
Tisvaya with an ancient talisman,
hunting for me when I couldn't even say, *"vicar."*

  "Your letters were deeply lovestruck,"
She chose as her first sentence and my first register.

"I help the spies, and camouflage men,
provide them with water and fodder,
and I never shy from learning new skills.
Your past paramour,
a person of was-valour,
is ex-communicado.
Should've stayed with you."

"What?
Why should I believe you?"
I barked, but I sounded like a beat-up mouse—
too fragile to raise decibels,
too vigorous to deal with emotions frothing beneath the surface.

"A coup prevented.
The sanctity of the written word,
the fortune of common men,
the innocence of girlhood—
all would have fallen
if the black-necked battalion had flagged the constitution.

Your past paramour,
would have wiped away half the world,
along with you."

"Should I be jovial or mournful?" I asked.
                                             "How about hopeful?" she replied,
                                                    winking a smile.
"I have nothing left to hope for,"
I moaned, as she pressed the vedic concoction against the plaster.

> *"I will not die but live,*
> *And will proclaim what the Lord has done,"*
> recited she, the psalm 118:1.

"I have nothing left to proclaim,"
my shrugged self said.

> *"You will. I will see to it,"*
> proclaimed the stewardess princess.

A fortnight of caregiving,
quartets, psalms, and sermons,
healing along with falling,
all anew.

To top it off—
the lotus pond,
at the nexus of our shared seclusion,
unburdened by wild weathers or barbed wires.

For I found depth in deprivation bottomless.

Resurrection post crucifixion.
Lord sent a steward-princess,
affirming the laid laws of God-physics.
A fountain inside me, but I carried an empty bucket.
Miracles deep in the mind-deserts do occur,
but dwell in the improbable and the invisible.

The Lord grants a coup,
more than once in a blue moon,
and I dispelled the false truth.
For it was me—unbeknownst—who did most of my abuse.

Long story short…

A Dead Man's Bucket List

Songyee Park

E unha woke as she was dragged ashore, wet jagged rocks scraping against her back. Her chest caved then erupted as she coughed repeatedly, sputtering back to life. She purged mouthfuls of water and the crisp air clawed at her lungs.

"Took you long enough."

She sat up slowly.

"Yeon?" she rasped.

Yeon was exactly how she last remembered him eleven years ago, barely seventeen, jittering, in his school uniform a size too big because he never got the chance to grow into it. His pleated pants were damp and clinging to his knees. His eyes were bloodshot and the bandages wrapping his left palm needed changing.

She looked up at the torrent that exploded over the edge. Like heavy machinery, it drummed the ground beneath her feet, but the spray was gentle, hanging droplets on her brows and lashes.

It could've been any waterfall on Earth, but she knew exactly which one. She'd been saving up for this trip ever since she first heard about it on her morning commute.

"Truly, a force of nature," the voice on the radio had commanded, thick with reverence. "Skógafoss. The sky had split wide open, pouring the heavens straight down to earth—"

"Are you okay?" Yeon asked, as he squeezed the water from his pants.

"Where, what is this?"

"Whatever you want to call it. You're dead."

"This, you can't be real."

The boy shrugged. "I'm as real as I can be, I guess."

Water glistened in the low Nordic sunlight. Air hung heavy, with the musk of minerals, melted snow and stubborn grass. Mist rose from the base, reflecting an incomplete rainbow.

Yeon picked up a rock the size of his fist and threw it into the curtain of water. He picked up a smaller one and threw it sideways, trying to make it skip. It sank after two jumps.

Eunha watched him, bewildered, as she recalled moving out of their forgettable fishing town right after high school. Up until the last day, Yeon's ghostly presence followed her around. He was a tired face printed on cereal boxes, laminated on posters at bus stops, and crinkled between old newspapers that her mother repurposed, to wipe down dewy windows in the morning.

Auntie, Yeon's mother, had come by to say goodbye. Their moms sat in the living room, chatting between tangerines while Eunha packed her suitcases for Seoul. They sighed, reminiscing about their own school days, gushing over trot singers and Elvis-wannabes. Auntie seemed better, but her smiles never quite reached her eyes again.

Yeon searched her face now with the same hooded eyes. Tired with her silent anguish, he hobbled over to a patch of grass and sat down. She followed, sitting close.

"Did anyone find my body?" he asked. She shook her head.

They really tried. Everyone did, except for the boy's own father, who continued to gamble away his last belongings over Go-Stop. They scoured through every beaten mountain pass, deer-nibbled cabbage fields and fish-gut stinking harbors along the southern shores of Gyeongsang-do. After each attempt, the adults gathered around for makgeolli to keep morale high, but no amount of sweet rice wine could wash away the sobering reality that they were looking for bones by then.

"Yeon, where the hell did you go? What happened to you?"

"Went to Yeosu. Fell off the dock near the lighthouse."

Eunha swore. They never searched that far. They should've.

She turned away from him and the waterfall. There was a small farm in the far distance, complete with a picturesque barnhouse next to square patches of harvest. She thought it was wheat or something, but when she stared at it for longer, she could see that they were flowerbeds of money, with petals made out of the yellow fifty-thousand won bills.

Nearby, she could only recognize a white camping car in an otherwise empty parking lot. It was something she might've rented if she went on that road trip around Iceland. A gray ribbon of cracked asphalt wrapped the landscape, stapled down on a carpet of stubborn moss, needled with jagged outcrops of volcanic rock.

The absurd landscape was all her doing, according to Yeon, who tried to explain. "I don't know how this place works, but if you really want something, the earth gives it to you."

The quiet countryside. Money. A camping car. Empty roads. Yeon, in the flesh. Earth had become her very own movie set, minus the camera and crew. No witnesses nor bystanders to criticize her every decision. So here they sat, untouched by time, in a dollhouse the size of her perceivable universe.

"You wanted to see this waterfall?" he asked, unsure, waving his arm at the scenery around them. "What's next? What else did you want to do?"

"Does it matter anymore?"

"It's fun. Cathartic. You won't believe what I got up to, before you arrived."

Animated, he recounted his adventures. Yeon went to the moon and looked for rabbits. He adopted a tiger, named him Cat, and rode him up and down the Hallasan peaks and valleys. When he was afraid of the dark, but itching to go for a swim, he filled a river with glowing jellyfish. They stung and tickled him.

After all the childish escapades, he went to art school. Nameless people shook his hand, asked him for photos, filled his shelves with awards, and lime-lighted his pieces on museum pedestals.

"Mom, she was so proud of me, showing me off, telling everyone how awesome," he trailed off. "How awesome, I could've been, I suppose."

"I'm sorry," Eunha interjected.

"For what?"

She pointed to his bleeding hand. "And for everything I said."

"In the art studio?"

She nodded. The last time they saw each other, she found him in one of the dusty backrooms, skipping lunch, and chipping away at the limestone, his hair, cheek, and forearms powdered like fresh dough. After a heated argument, she had rejected him and pushed him too hard. He fell, cutting his hand on a chisel. A few days after that, Auntie called, sobbing, looking for him.

'I found him. He's fine.' She wanted to tell her now.

"It's fine." Yeon picked at the bandage. "So? What did you want to do? What else was on your wishlist?"

"I don't know. I can't even remember what I was doing before I–" she paused, lost for words. "Before you died," he finished for her.

The answer should've been easy. There were many things left undone. After moving to Seoul, earning a business degree, and barely landing an underpaid job, Eunha spent years suffocating in an office flooded with white lights and angry sighs. An uncomfortable encounter early in her career prompted her to cut her hair short and dress plainly, hoping to blend into the background. Too often, she had no time for a proper meal, resorting to instant ramyeon over the sink. And over the years, her confidence and self-worth shrunk to fit her paycheck. She went to sleep with a dull ache in her neck and woke before sunrise, wishing she could call in sick, just so she wouldn't have to do it all over again.

There had been good moments, however, that made her life bearable. The Christmas she spent in Prague with her sister, wrapped in the warmth of mulled wine and candlelight. The small vegetable garden on her veranda, where worm-repelling marigolds bloomed in the summer. The quiet triumph of finally perfecting her mother's *doenjang–jjigae* recipe after weeks of trial and error.

And Yeon had too few of that.

"C'mon, Eunha," Yeon prodded, stretching his legs out in front of him. "I've been bored for so long. Who cares what you did or didn't do when you were alive? None of it matters anymore."

Eunha watched him stretch his arms above his head. He was thinner and paler than she remembered, like a photograph left out in the sun too long. She had eleven more years than he did. Eleven years that slipped by against her wishes. She thought of him when the seasons changed, when flower pollen made her sneeze and when she struggled to walk on sleeted sidewalks. He was an ache that came and went, a dull, persistent ache that she couldn't shake.

She cupped his hand and unwrapped the wet bandages. His finger joints were callused and pebbled from all the hammering. A deep red groove dug into his palm end to end, raw and defiant against his sparsely dotted life-line.

She watched the fresh capillaries slowly stitch across the cut. Pink skin fluffed up the crevice like blooming cotton balls.

Eunha had missed him for a lifetime. Much like Skógafoss and its downpour, he had always been her in-*yeon*[1], perhaps, an unrealized dream at the bottom of her list, never crossed off.

"I suppose that's a start." He smiled, looking down at his hand, good as new.

"I'm burnt out. I don't want to do anything right now." Eunha groaned, letting out a long sigh, exhaustion settling deep into her bones.

"Tell me more of your crazy stories. What else did you do?" She added, falling back onto the grass. She looked up at the spotless sky. She could stare straight into the sun, without it hurting her back.

"Eunha, I need to tell you something. Before you got here," he paused, "I wished for something terrible. I felt so alone. I missed you and wanted you here with me." Eunha stiffened. Yeon exhaled, still looking down at his hand.

"I was angry," he defended. "You were smart, top of the class. You probably went to Seoul, got a nice job, had a family, lived a perfect life, while I was stuck here, drowning in nothing. And like I said, the earth–it listens to you."

Her voice came out hoarse. "What are you saying?"

"You were driving and there was an accident," he mumbled, as he rubbed his face with his healed hand. Eunha felt her heart beating faster.

"Don't get me wrong. I felt horrible. I regret it so much."

The sky fractured. Thunder cracked overhead, a jagged wound splitting through the open air. The first raindrop struck Eunha's cheek like a needle, sharp and cold. Then another. And another. Water erupted from above, as if Skógafoss itself had exploded on top of her. It crashed against her in a deafening roar, hammering her body.

"Eunha, are you ok?" Yeon shouted against the storm. "What's happening?" The memory of her last living memory trickled through her pores, pooling beneath her ribs.

She was driving back home after a visit to Radiology, struggling through the thunderstorm. A woman shrieked, laughing on the radio. She turned it off. She tried to keep steady, listening to the ticking metronome of the emergency lights. A truck cut in front of her and she swerved too late. Metal folded around her. She waited, hanging in her seat, crumbled and calm. She watched the storm pass by, pressure-washing the reddened concrete. A pair of gloved hands tugged at her ruined blouse and towed her out—a cold, battered bag of meat.

Eunha bolted upright, fingers locking onto Yeon's shirt, fists twisted in the fabric. "Was it you?" she seethed, "the truck and all?"

"What are you saying?" Yeon recoiled, eyes blinking away the water. "I just imagined it, that's all! I would never, in real life," he admitted, "want to let anything bad happen to you!"

"What else?" She was trembling, drenched under the freezing water. Her words spilled out between ragged breaths. "What other horrible things did you curse on me? In this fucking limbo?"

The possible revelation clawed at her lungs. She wondered if she could suffocate and die again. Had it all been him? The exhaustion, the loneliness, the missed chances? Had her life been shaped, not by chance, but by Yeon's bitter *han* [2] that crawled out of his watery grave?

"I swear, Kim Eunha, I don't know what's happening, but I'm sorry," he begged, holding onto her hands gripping him. "I'll go drown myself in that waterfall if that makes you feel better."

Eunha was too tired now, even for anger. She sank down onto the muddy ground. The shower beat against her head and back, relentless. She let go of his shirt. They were already drowning in should-haves.

Eventually the storm passed. Skógafoss remained reverent, forever flowing. The rainbow, still incomplete. The barnhouse, still picturesque.

The sky, still spotless and blue. The earth, still devoid of any living thing, except for Eunha and the boy she still missed.

They sat there for a long time. Their clothes dried and Yeon was no longer wiping tears away from his cheeks. After a long silence, Eunha let out a shaky laugh.

"Road trip?" she finally suggested.

"Whatever you want to do," he agreed, standing up. He pulled her to her feet. They had a lot of catching up to do. And now, they had all the time in the world.

[1] Providence, fate. A Korean Buddhist concept that explores how relationships form over many lifetimes.

[2] A "feeling of unresolved resentment against injustices suffered, a sense of helplessness because of the overwhelming odds against one [...] and an obstinate urge to take revenge and to right the wrong." (credits: Suh Nam-Dong)

Death in the Daylilies

Poetry Collection

Alex Van Huynh

Alex Van Huynh

Death in the Daylilies

Human music – dropping bombs by dinner
And looking up, hatred at the sudden
Summer skies. Will they be left their gardens?
With every herb in frame?
All types of living pinned –
A young girl with her pins.
Death in the daylilies, stargazer, bred –
Thirty pale flowers as her own daughter,
Everyone's lover, nobody's mother.
Original children –
What first being would touch?
She at its perfect sphere
Kneels down etiolated limbs and just
As white-eyed motion, the evening notes bloom
Red, wet mouths like petals. *Express! Express!*
Second morning, bedded
Lawn – the shape her presence
Left hides a second root.

Ejecta

Both garden and gardener becoming,
Mutual roots from that iridic soil,
Their Lapsarian selves and ejecta –
A display for the female impactor.
It is the curious and absolute
When this temporary bloom, its pleasure
Spent, corrupts with procreative purpose
All along – the beastly eye, once loving,
Seeing senescence of form, grows hateful –
Like abhors like and today the shadow
Of the mammal moves through the arrangements
Still, deep noises of nature beginning
To portent and hear the hoofed heaviness
Of an animal in the desert-dark.
The dawn redwood's wood-winded motion draws
Rising rain and rose thunder – hurricane
Here! But what would happen if it was just
White noise machines on mistreated tables,
And from this, like a baby monitor,
Another human cry comes to exist.
By some future, the junco's naked boughs
Across the cold sun-spread snow – into these
Cloudless skies held up with wicker, ascends
Thinnest smokestacks high above once yellow
Larch and black spruce holding out their greenest.

Alex Van Huynh

The Principal Suffering

I am the speaker, who, as a child, when the goal was there,
A cinderblock out of place in nature, its weight and what
Life might lie beneath, as men they lined us up against them,
Knows in truth that what we dream we imagine while awake
As memory.

What then is to be done with intelligence?

This is my suicide gargling, choking out the Lord's Prayer,
A spring from the mouth upturned with a mixture of water
And black hair – an intention without medium – silent
Penance, the blasphemous vibration quieted, for all
Words are profane.

What places, western, eastern, mark
With two facing definitions,
Ignoring by the roundabout
Their own redefining? Names change –
Identify! I see them unidentifiable,
And so, imagining love,
We command: "Act for me baby!"
Opening the other's body –

Drawers! Drawers!
Just belts for appearances
And means of a belted neck,
More pleasure and most final –
Oxygen away! And yet
This won't stop the point of view.
The principal suffering –
A gun to the principle!
Unblinking, the accident
Changes and devils come quicker than the first responders.

Kill you, keep you with me, reader –
Whatever you understand of me, this is your halting
Problem – body-black oracle
And tape of one's thoughts – blue spotlights on sets of skies, the show
To sounds of continual cheers –

Arena! Arena! Arena! Abject,

I level my face – there is no expression but your own.

Drop Ceiling-Sky

Clean skin – man and woman's highest desire
Divided – a dream-house, drop ceiling-sky
Above, proof of life cut on the keyboard –
Both our wrists branded and banded gold – what
Possible memories could be prepared?
I imagine her saying "I hate you."
By caged light, iron-cased incandescence,
Her breathing is transparent – tears for my
Wet-faced rain and mirror-wasted beauty –
The alfear by other boys allayed now,
With chattering teeth, speech-extended gape,
His braying face in bed. The cigarettes
We take, secrets slowly burning, light smoke
Like others who have shared them, each a sun's
Single color, dimmer in the other's
Infinite overhead – here the finite
Body, its variegated scratches.

Alex Van Huynh

Black and Lighthouse

Shorelines and speakers, their mutual ontogenies –
New Jersey solid cadet and emerald,
Refractions of summer lay Aegean ceramics,
And off the Cape Peninsula sky-wash swells
Of surface strobe and surge on screen, until finally –

Dive into her!

Tread! Tread! Dark water! That booming boundary –
The tops take sorry Captain Douglas
In the zero-stillness down.
All that I am, my simple set of actions
Inked upon the zoetrope – black and lighthouse
Circulate the filmed scene, collimated sun
Arcs and arcs around me across crests and troughs
Of child-shaped boxes.
To cope, one watering eye colorizes half white, half red seas,
Stained glass to the single insufferable light –
Beg for the dream! *Doldrums! Doldrums!*

Salt calls my breath! Sand-open origin –
Bright seagull shadows o'er the small whitecaps,
Ocean and air in their marrying force –
The surf has been humbled – kiss me earth-maid!
In the conchoid's spiraling mystery,
Panic-officiated, sanctified
Pain, human but bearable miracle!

Beaut

Michelle Chen

You don't like it when people make friends with people just because of how they look so you keep quiet when Sharon Lee sidles up to you in sixth grade social studies class and asks if you have something to write with. I'm biracial too, she tells you while you hand over your box of jelly pens. I'm not, you say.

Every day after that she smiles and waves at you from across the room even when Ms. Crock is watching. You let her keep the purple pen and her notes to you are glittery lavender all month. You find out she loves books just as much as you do and the reading chart is the greatest event all year because neither of you ever knows who will win. Every twenty books you log for class you get a toy from the class jar, and by December your bedroom in northern Queens is clogged with little foam puzzles and squeeze balls and mood-change pencils that spill out into the living room hallway sometimes and vanish when your foggy gray cat without a name chases them into the dark at night.

At the annual middle school dance you dart in between uptight girls in tank tops smelling of sweet tea who refuse to dance and groove like fireworks (Katy is the confident older sister you never had) and boys who you refuse to talk to due to still being scared of their size and loudness and badness in class. The skeptical Korean and studious black boys have snuck into the cafeteria and hooked up a small TV and Wii system to play Mario Kart.

The Italian boys are goofing off in the playground with a bag of water balloons that they fill from the fountain that Sharon once poured an entire thermos of old soup into from a two-day-old lunch. You watched each ball puff up from the second floor homeroom window that afternoon, like the throat of a bird from a nature documentary that you saw on PBS during the one hour it is on TV, even though PBS Kids has become really tempting with their new episodes of Curious George which you still love and hate so much you swear your heart split in two. One for the mature you and one for the you who wants to be taken care of for infinity.

Across the room you spot Sharon in a jean jacket near a table heaving with cheese balls, fruit gummy packets, and soda bottles, loading her teeny paper plate with food. She turns around and you are struck by her polish: the swirl of a black choker around her throat, illuminated (new SHSAT word!) brown eyes, new daubs of navy on her nails that dig through the bounty.

You are glad both of you are still scared of makeup and tweezing. She shows you a photo of her cat on her Blackberry phone, and you burn with unexpected happiness at how it could be mistaken for your own cat's sibling: same moody gray fur, eyes like someone poured a tall glass of lemon juice and peppered it with a mug of brown sugar before anyone thought of stirring it.

You want to show her a picture of yours but your parents haven't given you a phone yet, and it doesn't matter because Cotton Eye Joe starts blaring from the speakers. Ms. Crock had rapped her desk to bring the class to attention one day early spring, and declared that learning the dance together would be a life skill for living in America, "like speaking English, or paying taxes once you get old enough," so you follow each other onto the dance floor and intertwine your steps with each other. Both of you are laughing by the time the room forms a conga line, especially at the few skeptical Korean and studious black boys who grab onto the snake and make exaggerated arm gestures -- one's clammy hand sinks into your back and he waves the other like he is in a rodeo as you clutch the ends of Sharon's jean jacket and dream of summer.

Next fall a new group forms -- Sharon, Angela, Rachelle, and you. None of you ever really think of visiting each others' houses after visiting Rachelle's mansion. It becomes the place where everything seems to begin and end. Her home makes your bedroom in northern Queens seem not north at all, fifteen minutes on the MTA bus before it bumps onto a street parallel to the ocean.

It is the place where you meet to go to crowded birthday parties at Chuck E.Cheese's, skiing on winter break, bowling on vacation Friday nights, and movies at AMC theaters. Except after a couple of trips, either you and Sharon get bored and go back to your books, or your families stop taking you. Angela and Rachelle are the type who roll their eyes at

Shakespeare and know exactly what kind of life they want. You still all hang out at school, though.

"Don't think about all that, it doesn't matter what other people have," your mother says sharply. "Now, come help me take this bed apart." You are embarrassed that neighbors and passersby can see you, two Chinese women kneeling on a mattress base in a tiny weed-ridden yard ringed by rusted wire fencing. But that changes when your mother gets out the steel tools - you want people to see you two at work, dazzlingly capable, muscles swelling behind your oversized shirts.

You will always remember this, the first time you feel truly useful. Together you cut through layers of plastic wrap and tape that have protected it from rain and mold, then into the veneer fabric, buds of yellow foam opening up in unexpected places. Prying apart the wooden frame piece by piece, puzzling out where you could use the hammer and pliers, and stacking them together to tear out nails from tail to stern. You are surprised at how easy and hard it is to break it down.

Through a silver fog of dust your mother tells you to hammer in every single nail so they lie flat along every block and beam.

"Are you just making more work for me?"

"If you're gonna do something, always do it right. These nails are a hazard to everyone -- delivery workers, garbage truckers, us! If you're careful, and patient, we can all live in harmony."

That was how she raised you.

One day at lunchtime you see Sharon picking at her lunchbox at a wide white cafeteria table, alone. Another day when chorus is over and you are walking past double doors you see a flicker through the reinforced window -- Sharon, crouching at the base of the stairs and shaking her head. You watch it wobble back and forth and the longer it goes on the more you feel like you need to go, get a snack from the vending machine or ask a teacher about homework, anything but watching a girl seizing up alone in a half-lit stairwell.

Remember what your mother told you. When you see her pale face next, you run to catch up with her. "Hey, I'm with you," you manage to murmur as the sixth, seventh, and eighth grades spill through the stucco hallway after fifth period. She doesn't say anything but looks relieved. Her illuminated eyes are still, even now, illuminated.

Someone, Angela or Rachelle or one of their more distant friends, has seen you talking to her, and that is your undoing. In the crowded hallway you feel a sharp flick on your shoulder, a warning made physical. An arm turns you around, and as you meet the girl's eyes your stomach drops at the harshness of her frown, aimed at Sharon who fades away into the crowd.

Over the next couple of days, you linger at the edge of Angela and Rachelle's group, picking up bits and pieces about Sharon at their full lunch table, while waiting for classes to begin, or lining up at the gym. It all comes to you like alien radio chatter.

"She yelled at a teacher -"

"She never paid me back after the Scholastic book fair -"

In your mind, you can hear their thoughts even when they never say them out loud after that, feel scowls radiating in corners, like you've suddenly gained x-ray vision and hearing out of nothing but your fear of them. When you retreat into your books their voices follow you too.

"She's too nice -"

"She's hard to influence -"

A group of sharks parting around the hull of a sunken ship. *Two* sunken ships.

You fend off glares the rest of the year, until the next invitation to Rachelle's mansion.

While playing Uno over winter break, you watch Rachelle stroke Sharon's cat, which she brought over to entertain everyone before Rachelle's dad is supposed to drive you to see Frozen. He feels guilty, you think, that her mother is away so often in Taiwan drafting up packaging designs. You and Sharon trade school library books, vowing to return them for each other. Both of you watch Rachelle, Angela, and five other girls throw cards around the circle and yell and laugh, but you feel like she is your tether, and your eyes graze each others like passing ships, which comforts you.

Snow petals down across the windshield as the minivan hurtles into the night. When you hand your tickets to the usher with greasy blonde hair, he looks at you, blinking wetly, and keeps looking at you when you walk down the hallway. You even turn around a little to see if he is watching, and he watches back and smiles like your motion is nothing to him, that it holds no shame of suspicion.

Inside the theater, the soft black darkness soothes you as Rachelle's dad passes around Ziploc bags of M&Ms, popcorn, and jelly beans. Snow bursts across the screen as you lean back, filling your belly like an empty cave, and when Anna is racing through terrible cracking ice to look for her sister it takes a while for you to realize that there is no one in the seat beside you.

It's only when the clouds part and each moment becomes a bright castle scene that you manage to get up, empty bag slipping in the grease of your hands. You slink out of the dark and into the rosy light of the hallway, and, turning the corner, you see Sharon standing beyond the concession stand with a man in a brown jacket. Behind them both, through the glass doors, is a silent police car, rivulets of red and blue leaking between their bodies.

Even the concession stand worker has looked up from her phone, wiping down crumbs of popcorn to hide her sneaky glances. The man talks and talks to her, but Sharon doesn't move, doesn't seem to even breathe. Finally, she walks down the carpet towards the car and from here you think you see a dark flash of pity on the man's face, the edges of his mouth turning into little prongs, before he opens the car's backseat door for her and she gets in.

"Sharon's a liar. She means bicultural not biracial," Angela says, bringing out a platter of foamy-to-the-touch shrimp crackers from the kitchen on Rachelle's sixteenth birthday. "She grew up on Long Island out on Montauk in a Catholic school until fifth grade. At least that's what I saw in the poem she wrote that won the city festival prize. I can't believe it won when it literally says she's embarrassed. Can you believe that? Embarrassed about badly dressed Asians? Like, the fuck?"

She talks in a quick light voice that lands these insults like parachutes instead of rockets.

Your stomach twinges as you shake your head along with them as Rachelle brings out her own cake from the freezer. Peals of cold whipped cream curl around a constellation of strawberries and a hard base of matcha ice cream—specially customized by Taipan Bakery.

It's only years later that you realize that you and the others became her family, against loneliness. None of you four have any siblings, so you nurture each other, even though you've been feeling out of the loop lately from turning down study sessions for AP Chem and last break's skiing trip. You still want to write poems and articles and stories, but you have Googled variations of "Sharon Lee," "Sharon Lee writing," and "Sharon Lee high school poetry" enough to know that she has become even more intimidating to you than some of the white girls who had English majors for fathers or whose mothers worked as a newspaper's editor-in-chief.

After dinner, when people are packing up, you notice the gray cloud hovering around your ankles for the first time that night, and you throw it chunks of mayonnaise tuna left over from sandwiches. Rachelle's been keeping it safe all this time - the cat has plenty of room to roam here and she's always wanted another pet ever since she killed her tropical fish from overfeeding in middle school.

Fur stands on end between your fingers. The moment Rachelle approaches you with a couple boxes of leftover lo mein for the journey home, the cloud flickers and vanishes down the basement stairs.

John is nice enough to you, and mean enough to you at the right times, that when he fastens the corsage around your wrist it seems like prophecy, the ribbon closing above your hand and feeling like a bite of warm chicken rice.

By prom night you face each other like boxers in a ring, across the tilting downtown subway car. Rachelle's sick of sparring with her father, Angela is bubbling over with excitement out of fear that after her acceptances people will think she's a stuck-up bitch if she acts any other way, and you are content just being there as always, like a listener tuning into two radios while their dates gaze out the subway door windows into the darkness.

On the dance floor you realize you are sitting smack in the middle of a long beautiful web, stemma radiating out toward each individual, so that if you collapse someday they would hold you tight, a noose of social interactions and excellent hugs, messages in all caps saying "GUESS WHO I JUST RAN INTO" and "text me when you get home."

Later, when you are looking at each other in the bar bathroom mirror, fixing hair and chatting about how a date looks so bad trying to grow a mustache, you see your friends' presence glowing like polished quartz, hair consuming light like swatches of backstage curtain. A cloud wafts through your mind for the rest of the night, and you turn down a waiter offering you sparkling water. A flicker of gladness in John's eyes when you hold him close, looking over his shoulder for Cotton Eye Joe instead.

After Angela gets into Yale, you return to her Instagram which has the link to her Tumblr called Golden Ratio, which has 2,000 followers, one for nearly each year all of Western civilization has been around. But it's still less than half of all Chinese years.

On goldenratio.tumblr.com, after scrolling past photos of meticulously arranged stationery, morning coffee and croissants, and wooded scenes, you find her most popular quote:

If you're not moving forward, you're moving back.

That night you have a nightmare you don't remember but that leaves you parched. You search up an old Instagram that confirms what you think you already know—Sharon with a big group of girls in paint splattered shirts, holding a photo booth picture at a Mets game, a caption saying, "Thank you to every member of City Squad for teaching me so much about life."

In college, some of the other students startle you with their behaviour—throwing candy wrappers on the ground, stuffing them inside desks, and later in the depths of night, leaving behind spilled beer cans in the parking lot after tailgates. The cans are left for cars to dodge around as the sun rises, and crunch underneath their wheels as campus parking spaces fill up in the morning.

You remember what your mother told you and are tired of this thoughtlessness, so you move to Brooklyn, attracted to the clean rows of brownstones that look like the setting sun on fall leaves just about to crisp. Halloween has become cold and damp as an adult, and there is a chill inside your little brownstone rental, which you split with a roommate, so you make a trip home, taking the long route by subway into Manhattan and Flushing.

Half your high school friends have turned into acquaintances, all your acquaintances have turned into strangers, and John has turned into men who talk too excitedly to you on your undergrad dorm floor, who have a hard shine in their eyes while taking your morning bodega coffee, a shard of light that you are also privileged to see when taking the subway back past nine p.m. after overtime in the library.

You maneuver yourself in line on Main Street for pork buns and emerge with a warm white plastic bag knitted between your fingers. Something—the sunlight, or the enormous afternoon crowd crisscrossing the intersection—steers your eyes toward the propped-open door of a shop, which you look through like a one-way mirror.

A slice of face emerges: it's Sharon, trying to steal the miniature red-eared turtles in Mr. Ling's shop. She is a shadow ducking to the linoleum floor the moment Mr. Ling and his assistant are in the back restocking the new shipment of potted plants.

The black face mask and her long dark hair, streaming out like the tail of a wild mule, mean she could pass for any new immigrant in the heart of Flushing. You want to beg at the soles of her Adidas-encased feet, to grab her arm so that it pulls out of her socket with a nasty crunch, in a bitter motion like snapping a joint off a Harbin ice sculpture, upon which the cold air of her soul would pour down onto your cheap shoes, as per convection current rules in Biology 332, the highest class you took before you quit because, fuck, you really don't want to work that hard.

You want to plead, "Don't make us look bad in front of the blonde woman and toddler boy out front fondling the miniature bamboo plants."

Your own roommate in Brooklyn is a white girl from Ohio wearing a jade bracelet who already called you a thief and a slob on a yellow Post-it note on the bathroom mirror when you weren't as tidy as Marie Kondo in her Netflix subscription, nor made eye contact as much as she wanted you to when she upended the apartment looking for her cherry-lime-flavored vape.

It turned out to be tucked inside her boyfriend's backpack when he commuted to Columbia Law School that morning, but not before she upended your laundry hamper and let out an "argh" that could have been a scream except good girls don't scream at Asian women unless they're thieves and slobs.

You step into the shop as she flees with her face down, dropping your bag on the ground behind you to cover the noise and moving into Mr. Ling's line of sight.

"I'm really sorry," you say, and pass over six dollars – three for the broken succulent pot on the counter and three for a large cup of tofu pudding with sugar syrup.

It's been a while since you stepped foot into the Li family home, but you're happy to accept their Friendsgiving dinner message.

"I've found her," you tell them.

Faces look up from plates of roast duck, cranberry salad, and sushi.

"Really? How is she? What's she doing? Is she still writing? I heard she went to a community high school in Harlem or something."

And for a moment you are refreshed by their sense of community, thinking about how you were startled by lunch groups with women who talked a lot more harshly and out loud: "I worry about her because she's not making good choices," someone says viciously. "He's a jerk," a brunette adds to her friend in front of the cashier. "You have anything to add?" Andrea, the kindest, speaks to you and smiles, secure in her kindness before moving on. You don't know which is more hurtful, their public sharpness or the Li group's private abandonment. Sharon has always been quiet, though not as much as you, and you wonder if that made it easy for her to vanish, so that the whole of her is now remembered as rumors and Google searches.

"She wants her back. The cat." You listen carefully for any resentment.

"Where's she living?"

"She just told me to meet at the Starbucks, she didn't tell me where she lives."

"I'm taking her home to her."

"Yeah, I'm taking her home."

You think that the basement of a mansion would be different from your own small house plastered with weather-blackened panels, but you spy a moth lingering around the corner bathroom. It reminds you of your own undergrad basement days, living with your mother to save money -- moths in the summer, beetles in the spring, heater in the winter, centipedes in the fall.

Out of the shadows, a cat leaps, like a blown plastic bag, out from underneath a ping pong table. You spring back and crash into a defunct tank, which topples over spectacularly, black machinery and dead fish ghosts pouring out of its hollowed out insides. When you turn and lift everything back to its old position, like your mother taught you, the cat is already nipping at your ankles.

You gather up the cat, who looks like your cat's sibling, in your arms and walk upstairs. There's not much you and Rachelle and Angela can talk about anymore, with them breezing through MCAT textbooks and your own applications to a state college's graduate school of social work languishing online. But you don't really need to talk, do you?

"Do you want more food? You can get the Nanjing salted duck from the refrigerator."

"Take all you need. Do you want some fruit?"

You're grateful, until the cat lets out a meow in her decade-old carrier.

"We'll miss you." Rachelle pinches gray cloud cheeks. "Say hi to Sharon for me."

You get exactly where you need to go. Your mother is sleeping in a room perfumed with clementines, so you put the food in the fridge. The videos on the bus ride flicker through your mind—cats smelling each others' blankets, pacing around a door underneath which they can see another's shadow, staring at each other through cracks and crevices and hard wire.

What would you have to talk about? You want to call out to Sharon, about books and clothes, but you are afraid these topics are too childish, too useless for a thief in foster care stealing wild animals. You want her to find her way back to the mansion that was never yours or hers, but only out of her own want. You want to shoot over a Facebook message that her cat misses her even though that's a lie, the cat had eventually warmed to Rachelle, as if any one of the Li group could be interchangeable with one another. You even type out, "lost cat", into the message bar, and then close the app entirely. Really, what is she to you but gossip and a name on the internet?

But tonight the cat lives here, in the dark, where no one comments on her beauty, her yellow eyes like cross sections of tossed beach crystal. She yowls, and from down the hall behind your closed bedroom door you hear your own cry back. Her cat's the unstable one, you think, growing up with Sharon in a harsh environment like that, then moving into a stranger's house where people came and went at strange times, strange people petting her while studying, shouting over cards and games with little neon pieces to bat under the sofa, cutting spare ribs and cake and neck of goose.

So when you lift the carrier door the next morning, hand calm as an ice skating lake next to a sweet little backwoods cabin on one of Ms. Crock's reading reward American postcards, the extra prizes no one knew about unless they were there to see them in her desk while asking for more reading recommendations, you flinch when it's your cat who lunges forward with a wrinkled snarl, causing both their backs to curl like commas, as if, for all the world, wanting to tear each other apart.

Place

Amerasian

Poetry Collection

Lam Ho

Lam Ho

Amerasian

They never threw rocks at us in Vietnam,
but under a helmet, they saw the waves in my hair.
Mom said she still wondered about her father,
that faceless man who made her a demigod.

I am the daughter of the myth of old:
Her face, her figure, a mystery none of us could solve.
At the local McDonald's, she got soft serve for free.
Why? No one had ever seen a face like hers:
And in the mirror as I wash my hands, I remember
Ba resenting that white blood in our veins,
The reason Mẹ came here was because
she was the first of her kind—
 American-born father, Vietnamese mother, and I can't say
whether my mother's face is haunted or haunting,
but I will say she left a trail of broken hearts
passing on her treasured beauty—
an Old Testament to this New World.

How many threads cross between us now?
That time was so long ago,
yet that quarter of me still searches
in the night for the man we never knew.
When I see another Amerasian's face, I wonder:
What lonely places did you find in the night?
Did you embrace the ogling?
When did they stop throwing rocks at you in the street?
Did they ever stop?

Oceanic

I was twenty-eight when I learned why the ocean calls to me,
though it should have been obvious in the elementary insults
hurled at me in my Georgia youth — "Boat people"
or something like that, children pulling their eyes into slants.

I learned that in the ocean, escaping the war, my people
encountered pirates, drank their own urine, the women
stolen, never to be found again after leaving their homeland,
a place of beaches and rainforests—robbed for the white man's

Greed, still looming over us in America as we wash the feet
of those soldiers' children, perhaps our own half-siblings.
Once, as a child, I stood on the edge of the ocean and listened
as it roared. How silly to think we sleep to the white noise

Of an ocean crying out its secrets, acidifying with the bodies
thrown overboard, the boats so heavy that my people could
swing their fingers down and shave foam off the surface of the sea.
This is how my dad came to the States, by way of a body

In which he swam each day from the age of seven, ever transformed
by the marionette strings pulled by white faces thousands of miles away,
by a man whose hands look so unlike that of my father, more like
the hands of my aunt who still may never know who I am.

Lam Ho

Tent City

Tents
Were once
A symbol of comfort
Gorgeous in their simplicity
Like a wave of memories in nature,
Or that time we put one up in the lawn and
Watched *In Bruges* before kissing for the first time.

Now
Tents are
Something dangerous
Symbols of homelessness
Or violence unfolding on campuses
Which I used to see as safe havens where
Young Americans could protest injustices across the globe,
Like killing innocent families through starvation—slow and painful.

Atlanta:
We promised
Affordable housing
Along the Beltline, a lie.
And Emory, an institution meant
To build community, not break it, landed us
Damning headlines on international newspapers
For silencing students while calling them outsiders—
Everyone knows an outside voice is objectively dangerous.

Highways
Lined with tents
Tell the story of a city
Who failed its people: rents
Rising like Midtown buildings,
Welcoming outsiders while people
Who live in tents beg for money outside
My car window. I can't listen to bubblegum pop
Without feeling guilty because I have more than those
Who should own property in Atlanta, where Black excellence
Prevails. When did we decide to stack cards against those who pitched
The South, a tent of culture, food, music? Now I watch shameless
commodification, White faces stealing their craft, forcing them into tents
on the side of the road, out of sight.
But
I see.
So do you.

Lam Ho

Mono Lake

How could I forget the night we gathered
telling stories until the stars sharpened their edges
against an ever-darkening sky?
The way Yenyen's voice sounded as she told us
of those unlucky lovers separated by a galaxied sea.
I've always been a fan of tragedies
Perhaps because I haven't let go of the notion
love's only meant to last for short bursts—
more destructive than the supernova
that obliterates constellations with the morning sky.

So this is what I wanted: obliteration,
until I felt sun on my skin
and desires by night, like the undercurrent on
a lake pretending to be still.
Where do we store our yearnings
when the dark cloak no longer guards us?
Are our wants what comprise the pockmarks in our sky?
Is that why they shine brightest out of eyeshot?
When the moon blinks out for one night?

Is this why I may want something so far away?
Dead by the time I conceived of its possibility
but covet its opulence nonetheless?
I'm a rebel for dreaming and alone risk my life
for a glimpse of what could be.
Tonight clouds obscure my view
but their darkness shines in beautiful gloom.

I miss Mono Lake. But the sadness has lost its shine,
exploded into shards that pierced for 30 days
until the moon was new once again.
And she taught me the secret of Devotion.
She told me of the woman who wanders atop
lonely craters because her love was unbreakable.
You know what they do to women who love like that?

Airport Mesa

Walking along Airport Mesa,
I encountered an energy vortex.
It told me that my father had
left his homeland. Though it
did not say this part—I understood.
In this lifetime, I have been selfish.
I have chased boys but forgot
my old man fled the ocean, which
held him as a seven-year-old boy,
hardly aware that within decades,
he would swim to shore, confused,
and find his way to America.
I wept knowing this. Because I
have made a life of loving places
and I have no home. I know not
what it takes to leave one.

i40

Poetry Collection

KC Sisomphone

KC Sisomphone

i40

I spent many
years being shuffled
one way from west to east

then turning right around from east to west
we stopped
so I could switch somewhere exactly in between

the parents split
but visitation rights
made this gas station a portal

it was a threshold separating two half lives
two ages
like when I was a kid and now

here I would
eat sticky rice
around a table on the floor

here I would eat alone in my room
sometimes rice
but it was fried and tossed in sauce

here I would
pretend to live
with a tongue that couldn't speak

here I would pretend to live at all
safely anxious
behind a broken mask to look like nobody

my life is
a mixed bag
has been since I was born

I often find myself wondering how to reconcile
being both
half of my blood colonizer and half refugee

on that stretch
of highway between
these halves of me and me

I would look out of the passenger window
and dream
like maybe one day I could be whole

KC Sisomphone

2 min warning

grass with a fresh cut
curbs lined up
sun beams down on
after school
yard super bowls

draw the route on
the stitchless side
leather chalkboards
x's and oh damns
down, set

5 Mississippis before
they blitz you
fake inside, streak outside
Hail Mary pass
no two-hand touch
we bleed this

Randy Moss in
the end zone
spin the ball
like a globe and watch
the world grow up

when the sun went
down and it was time
to eat our food
sticky rice and papaya
salad, I just wish
they told us the game
would be
over

Grandma's House

these walls used to have
stripes, wallpaper I guess

they're painted white now
like the color of the steam

rising in the overhead light
while you fluff the rice

the sweet smell in the air
sticking in my nose

jeow, papaya, styrofoam plates
you washed after lunch

my hands are warm
and I can taste a tongue
that speaks across languages

Urang Sunda

Dea Ratna

Language is one of the things that makes us human. Language is also one of the reasons why I love and appreciate my culture so much, even though I was not born and raised in it.

Both of my parents are Sundanese, an ethnic group from West Java. They—like the other thousand-plus ethnic groups of Indonesia—have their own language, *Basa Sunda* or Sundanese. Both of my parents can trace their lineage at least four generations above as Sundanese. My mother grew up speaking *Basa Sunda*, having been born and raised in West Java. My father was not born and raised in West Java, but began learning later in life and became very fluent for the rest of his life.

My siblings and I? We were born and grew up in Jakarta and my parents never saw any reason to speak to us in Sundanese–so we only ever learned *Bahasa Indonesia*, or Indonesian. We all went to the States when my siblings and I were very young. Ever since, English has been the de facto language my siblings and I use to communicate with each other. There was never any natural space and time for us to use Sundanese–so we never learned.

At an extended family gathering, not long after we returned from the States and where I barely knew half the people in attendance, one of the elders gave a speech and began it as such:

"Biasanya kita pake Basa Sunda untuk sambutan, tapi karena ada empat orang disini yang tidak mengerti Basa Sunda, jadi terpaksa saya menggunakan Bahasa Indonesia."

"We usually do these speeches in Sundanese, but because there are four people here that don't understand it, I have no other choice but to use Indonesian."

Of course, the four people he meant were my siblings and I.

I felt embarrassed at being singled out like that. I knew he was doing it out of kindness, not pity. He wanted to include us, not embarrass us. But no matter his intention, it had a profound effect on me.

Do you know anyone who, when told they can't do something, does whatever they can to prove that person wrong? That was me after that gathering. I was determined to prove him wrong. I decided, no matter what, I would go to college in Bandung, the capital city of West Java. It didn't matter which college or what course, I would go to Bandung and learn Sundanese just to prove him wrong.

So that's what I did. I enrolled into the Bandung Institute of Technology (ITB) and signed up for the extracurricular *Lingkung Seni Sunda* (Sundanese Art Environment) group solely to learn the language. I didn't care about the art side of it. I just wanted to immerse myself in the most Sundanese environment I could find and this group was it.

Being surrounded by people who spoke almost exclusively in Sundanese yet had the patience to teach those who don't understand meant I learned Sundanese pretty quickly. I wasn't natively fluent and mostly only understood *Basa Sunda Kasar*, the informal version of Sundanese used only when speaking to friends. So, I did it. I proved him wrong.

But that's not all I learned from the group. As part of the new batch of members, I had to learn one of the arts and perform it in front of hundreds of people. As I gained more seniority in the group, I didn't perform as much, and instead became one of their main photographers. That meant I witnessed dozens of Sundanese dances and plays performed by my fellow students. And as I watched my friends dance, perform, and play various Sundanese instruments, I grew to love my culture and connect with it in ways that I'd never had the chance to before.

Proving my relative wrong turned into a secondary benefit. After around two decades of existing on this Earth, I could proudly claim myself as *Urang Sunda*. It wasn't the pure Sundanese blood that ran through my veins. It wasn't the gatherings with extended Sundanese families. It wasn't the frequent visits to various West Java towns to visit said relatives. No, it was entering a Sundanese group as an 'outsider' and truly immersing myself in the culture that made me connect with my culture.

That was over a decade ago. Unfortunately, I've lost my fluency since I moved out of Bandung. I can understand when people speak it and even unconsciously speak a few sentences here and there in Sundanese when talking with my relatives, but I can't carry a full conversation in the language. All that's left from my fluency is when I code-switch in front of my relatives and my Indonesian accent changes to a soft, Sundanese lilt, complete with Sundanese filler words like *sok, mah,* and *atuh.*

But I didn't lose the rest. I didn't lose my pride in being *Urang Sunda.* I didn't lose my appreciation for its arts or the giddy, nostalgic feeling that appears whenever I hear the familiar notes of the Sundanese suling and gamelan at a random restaurant. No matter what anyone else says, I am *Urang Sunda,* language fluency or not.

Thank you, Uncle, for starting your speech like that. It led me down a path that I would not have gone down otherwise. Thank you for lighting the spark that made me love the culture I come from. Thank you and you don't have to use Indonesian when speaking to me anymore. Just don't expect me to reply in fluent Sundanese.

The Hot and Cold Place

Poetry Collection

Zoe Parrott

Zoe Parrott

The Hot and Cold Place

It's nighttime but it's so bright.

Yeye and I are right next to a night market,

So I can distinctly hear people haggling over
the price of roasted pig ears.
Chop
The vendor cleanly removes the fish head.

The fish doesn't move, like it barely noticed.

Slurred mumbles find themselves cascading
out of my grandfather's mouth. He holds up 2 fingers.
He makes me point at what I want.
I want soup with a steamed egg, please.
I thank the vendor by forcing awkward vowels
through my teeth, American accent cementing my
tongue.
The neck strap for my glasses, slick with sweat,
swings precariously as I lurch forward,
sandaled feet slapping against the tiles. Yeye's
crooked finger
beckoning me towards the other side of the shop.

He asks if I want ice cream or shaved ice.

Yeye says it's my choice, but his eyes not so subtly

linger on the shaved ice.

I roll my eyes. Shaved ice, please.

Yeye wants red bean, but I don't care because I'm
too busy

side-eyeing the vendor across the aisle,
she's putting some lettuce on my soup.
I can't help but notice the glazed eye
of that fish she was cutting earlier, staring back at
me.

I don't like fish. She better not sneak any on. Please.

Plastic tray. Smooth bowls. Flaky shave ice.
Cracked leather seats. The soup is salty and hot. I
nibble on some lettuce
to ensure I don't burn my mouth.

You'll get throat cancer that way, Yeye says.

We share shaved ice
as the lights of the little shop melt themselves into
the city.
Sweet syrup and the artificial breeze of 10 fans
makes a pleasant night.

Goat Screams

Mir Aziz

Mir Aziz

April 11th

Do animals understand the idea of death? It's a question that crosses my mind often. There have been times where a trusting lamb in my arms, or an old cow lying on the grass, surely had no idea what was coming when I produced a knife and rested it against their necks. And there have been times where I have put goats on their backs, and they screamed and wailed in ways I did not know their vocal chords could produce, fear tangible and peril perceptible. Did they know what was going to happen? Or were they just uncomfortable? Or do they know that this is their end, and they cry in a desperate bid to avoid their fate? I cannot remember the first time I slaughtered a goat, but I do know that their screams did nothing to persuade me otherwise. I think it unnerves a boy, the first time he kills. But after that, it is simply routine. These thoughts came to me again this morning.

I heard goats screeching in the night. I thought it was an odd time to be slaughtering animals. But it came from Abdulhamid's house and, given his experience, I thought nothing of it and struggled to sleep. I do recall he tied up a few goats and planned to slaughter them that day, so it really did make sense. But when I awoke for morning prayers and walked by on my way to the mosque, I was forced to stop.

Abdulhamid was standing outside his house, staring at the trees. I came by him to do the same, admiring the sky as it began to turn from black to a brilliant flurry of purples. He didn't acknowledge me but it was no issue, for I thought we were but two men enjoying the company of nature, lost in the artistic mastery of the celestial bodies.

But I was wrong. Abdulhamid was lost in something else. His small red face was twisted in disgust, a vein visible across his bald head. His moustache-less lips were trembling, something that caused his salt-and-pepper beard to shake in the wind. Noticing his focus was elsewhere, I tracked his gaze. He was staring at great streaks of red across the walls of his house, at innards and intestines strung across the broken rice crops by the front of the house, just in front of his fish ponds. The smell was lost in the morning air, the stench of meat hidden by that of manure and standing water. I too became fixed on the butchery before us, and for a few moments he and I stood in silence, confused and shocked, attempts at answers disrupted by the placid ribbit of frogs. But no birds sang.

"Did the Sahib get drunk? Have his way with your animals?" I asked.

"No Britisher could do something like that," he said. His voice was low and quiet, and he did not turn to face me.

I knew it was a stupid question. How would a Britisher do something like this? And the current Sahib was not a cruel man. At least not from what we had seen.

"Did you see it?"

He said nothing.

"Did you see it?"

There was still nothing. I turned to leave until he said, "I did."

I swivelled back.

"It was a monster."

❧

Abdulhamid and I arrived at the mosque and we joined the congregation late. We rushed the second half of our prayer so that we would catch the men of the village before they all left. God forgive us. We told the men what had happened and their faces turned pale. I believe some were shocked out of self interest; I do recall Abdulhamid said he would distribute the meat of the goats, and many people were hungry and could not remember the last time they ate rice, let alone meat. But everyone was morbidly intrigued.

"Perhaps someone stole them." Shajul said.

I replied, "I thought so too. But one would have to be the world's worst thief to steal goats and leave the mess they made."

They agreed and there was more speculation.

Abdulhamid shouted above the crowd, "It was a beast!"

Everyone stopped talking and turned to him.

"What?" Shajul asked.

"It was a monster," he said.

Everyone was again left in silence.

"Did the thing leave any tracks?" Shajul asked.

"Not any that weren't covered by the rain or mist."

"And the goats are gone but parts of them are left?"

"Yes," said Abdulhamid.

Shajul pouted and squinted, his already almond-shaped eyes almost disappearing, and his thick purple lips expanding far beyond his cracked, black face. "It sounds to me that we have a cat problem. There's a leopard 'round here."

It was certainly a sensible suggestion to all of us present. I'd never seen a leopard attack but the scene did resemble some old stories my father had told me. But Abdulhamid was having none of it.

"It is no leopard," he insisted. "I've seen a leopard before and this isn't one."

"Well it can't be an actual monster."

"He is delusional," shouted one of the men. "He has seen a leopard slaughter his animals in the night, of course he is scared." This, again, sounded like a sensible suggestion to us.

The men all looked to me. "Gram sarkar," they said. "What do we do about this problem?"

The answer was clear, of course. "We shall hunt this thing, and give its pelt to Abdulhamid as a recompense for his goats!"

The men cheered me until Shajul asked, "How shall we hunt it?"

"We'll shoot it, of course!"

"Our guns are held by the Britishers," he pointed out.

"Remember,I was entrusted to keep mine," I replied.

"Will one gun be enough?"

Shajul is quite perceptive and sensible about most things and I think him to be a very clever man. But questions like this annoy me. Obviously, if you shoot something, it will die.

"It will be," I declared.

So we drafted a plan. We would head to the jungle and divide the men in two. A group of beaters would pound drums and scream to scare the cat out of the trees. If that doesn't work, we would set fire to the foliage and flush it out. In any case, the other half of the group would stab at the creature with homemade spears and swords, and I hoped to end it with a shot between its eyes. I planned to keep a handsome leopard pelt for myself, in honesty. Perhaps I would convince Abdulhamid to gift it to me. In any case, we'd do it in the morning.

April 12th

Today I have failed our village. I believe, in truth, I had failed us many times before. My grandchildren shall look upon my tenure and lament the legacy I leave them and the country. They shall remember me principally for two things, I think. Siding with the Britishers was and always will be a clear-cut choice in my mind. I know I will be judged unfavourably one day for it. But until this morning, it was a decision that had ensured the safety of our village and people. Now there is no safety. There is no security.

We assembled the men, twelve of us, just after the morning prayers. It was a beautiful morning. The sun was beginning to rise, and God had painted such a gorgeous painting on this canvas, with bright orange streaks accentuating soft pink and purple tones around the daybreak. The day was cool, and the smells of the farm and paddies were as pleasing as the scent of fresh dew. There was silence beside us, though the occasional splash of pond water reminded us that, though we on the land had a cat problem, the fish were completely impartial and continued on sniping for insects. We were all in good spirits, save for Abdulhamid who was still shaken. The men were jovial, and some had strapped knives to the end of staves, whilst others had brought their wood axes. I myself kept my father's sword on my waist, and his musket in my hand. And so we were off, chattering and laughing our way into the wilderness.

At the mouth of the jungle is where morale began to dampen. When we usually walked by, the air was loud with the calls of monkeys, the howls of dogs, songs of birds and whatever other babble its many inhabitants wished to express. But not this day. It was completely silent. I thought it a little strange that a single leopard should inspire such fear in all things. But other things still seemed to be in order. Tropical blooms tickled the nose, and the sweet smell of the jungle brought back fond childhood memories of exploration and adventure. But I had not been inside in a long time.

We entered and the world of the breaking dawn shifted to one of almost complete darkness. We tripped and fumbled over roots and foliage, unfamiliar with its current state, and were steadily brought to our feet and senses by those who depended more on its fruit and produce. The foliage was dense, and it was difficult to navigate the unending, night-impenetrable walls and forts of plants and trees that cloaked the land in perpetual darkness. Every snap of a twig became a deafening echo, thundering from all directions at once, disorienting us. We lost our groups as men fell into and amongst each other, confused as to where we were. We lost our groups, and the beaters and hunters became instead a babbling mess of confused and lost men, looking like a bizarre group of shaven apes to the denizens of the jungle.

I do not know when we lost the first man, for the initial losses were silent and unnoticed by us. It so happened that, after much struggle, we made our way to a clearing, and I noticed that three men were missing. So we turned back towards the foliage and called their names. There was no response. We heard the continued crunching of branches, but no men came from the jungle. Instead, a low, deep hum—no—growl came from the branches. My blood froze in my veins and my heart jumped into my throat.

It was here.

The leopard was here.

I raised my musket, loaded it and drew its hammer, as the other men readied their makeshift spears and axes. My pulse raced and I could hear and feel each laboured beat pounding through my body. I began to sweat. I began to tremble. But I was ready.

It pounced from the trees, landing upon Shajul. He screamed, but as soon as the sound left his mouth, the creature clamped down and tore off his head and throat with a crunch that seemed to splinter the world. Blood and brain sprayed into the air and upon us as Shajul's soul was savagely torn from his body.

And so we saw.

It was no leopard.

Before us was a hulking mass of twisted sinew, huge and awesome. Paws the size of a man's chest, each claw a dagger in its own right. Its body covered the horizon, orange fur with piercing black stripes. Its face was demonic: a white maw painted in gore, swords for incisors, between them a draping purple tongue. This was no leopard.

A cat for certain. One more ancient and fearsome than any other. One that our forefathers told us stories of, used as boogeymen and villains. One that had every feature and aspect of it crafted for the art of the hunt and predation. One that was, often to us, not even real, but a figment of an age and time long gone.

A Tiger.

It roared and we were turned to stone. I tried to move my arms but I could not, nor my legs, nor my head. Before me was death, both inflicted and manifest. My head pulsated and I could not breathe. At any moment it felt like my skull would burst from pressure. The creature pounced on another man and tore out his innards. My senses kicked back and I fired and hit it square in the side, but it did not even register the shot. It leapt upon the next man, knocking his face off with its paws. The remaining men began to scramble and I joined them.

I ran.

And I did not stop running.

We returned to the village, and I chaired an emergency council. I informed them of the situation, and that we were not able to retrieve the bodies for burial. Women cried and children were confused. I told them to set up wooden stakes around their houses, and to keep their animals locked up, and that children must not be left alone, and people should travel in groups. All standard defences against leopards.

I am not sure such things work well with tigers, though. I have just heard screams from Abdulhamid's property again. But I know they have no more goats.

Elegies of Nanjing

Poetry Collection

Diane Yang

Diane Yang

Elegies of Nanjing

(at the Memorial Hall of the Victims in Nanjing Massacre)

The gravel wasteland sinks into a deathly silence
Cicadas ensnared in the noose of judgment
Endlessly singing

Souls departed, with no tombstones or names
Reborn from their skeletal remains
Withered hands, reaching toward still waters

Bearings groan, wearied and mute
Blurred gray faces melting away
Mournful cries inscribed in the dust of wheels

In the blazing sun, the sundial-like flagpole
Scorches the hours away, burning down
The gazes of countless future successors

I have three hundred thousand[1] elegies to recite, yet words fail me
In December[2], every drop of ink was spent in weeping

[1] Three hundred thousand: The estimated number of victims of the Nanjing Massacre.

[2] December: The month in which the Nanjing Massacre took place.

I Saw You

Green sleeves and Ruqun[3] skirts,
Lost homeland, vague pain, and whispered words.
Across the garden drenched in dew,
Through this mist,
I saw you.

My heart uprooted,
As they marched, treaded and saluted.
Green plums[4] turn into bitter brew,
Through this liquor,
I saw you.

The Pronunciation of Pain

Pedestrians scurry to the crossroads of 36th Street,[5]
Where the broken accordion wails to the clamor of the train.
The gunshot drowned out the strum of a snapped string.
What, then, is the correct pronunciation of pain?

[3] Ruqun: A type of traditional women's skirt in Chinese Hanfu garments.

[4] Green plums: In classical Chinese poetry, "青梅" (green plums) is a metonym for a childhood sweetheart – someone who grows up together with another and later becomes their lover.

[5] 36th Street: On April 12, 2022, in the midst of Sinophobia caused by the COVID-19 pandemic, a mass shooting occurred on an N train arriving at the 36th Street station in Brooklyn, New York. The incident took place very close to the poet's residence in a nearby Chinese neighborhood.

Touch

Poetry Collection

Jiang Pu

Jiang Pu

Touch

This memory we hold in our hands
like flamed candles on the ship
shaped nights is unreachable—
what the ancient Chinese called
镜中花 flowers in the mirror,
水中月 moonlight in the water.

It is no longer louder than a creek
of frogs on a summer night, but a neighbor's cat
sneaking across my backyard. Soft
like an oven-fresh egg tart, its puff pastry snowed
with powdered sugar and cinnamon crushed
by time itself. The warm taste of a handful
of sun dropping from the lemon trees.

The rainy season is over. Moist memory linger
in the air, vibrating like a Tibetan
singing bowl. I can trace every layer of ego shed,
the way a butterfly traces its caterpillar molts:

your fingers once touched the petals
while mine touched the moonlight.

A Tribute to Bamboo （竹）

"I would rather dine without meat
than dwell without bamboo.
Without meat, one grows lean;
without bamboo, one turns mundane."
                    —Su Shi (1037-1101)

To bamboo, or not to bamboo?
There are runners and clumpers. Exercise caution
with those badass runners:

Unbarriered, they can grow lust-wild, disdain
property lines and boundaries, warzone friendly fences.
Unchecked, they can spread faster than infatuation,
shortly lose control, obsessed to pop up
from every crack.
Uncontained, they can enroot as hardy as true love,
willed to breach bricks, travel far and wide,
a real pain that may take years to remove.

When I bought a house with backyard bamboo,
some friends warned,
It's invasive! I would pull it out!
I wanted to say, *Nah there are root barriers.*
I've also got vigilant eyes.
Wait a second—

This stigmatized stranger is not
the beautiful bamboo I knew as a kid, back in East Asia,
where it is our dinner utensil, bed mattress,
and herbal medicine;
where we eat its shoots, drink its leaves, and wear its fibers;

where we use it to farm and fish, hunt and battle,
celebrate and entertain;
where we build, craft and furnish it
into houses and shrines, boats and rafts;
where our ancestors make flute and *dizi* from it,
write and paint with it, script books onto it, art-and-poetry it
as the spiritual truth of life:
a heart hollow from ego; a culm clean as virtue;
a Spartan upright with honor; a warrior stronger than steel;
a selflessness to amputate and regenerate;
a flexibility to bend but not break; a resilience to brave
harsh weather and flourish like hope;
a nobleman, a *junzi* that takes little and gives much;
an epitome of human-nature unity.

Ouch—this is too prosaic, too preachy: a digression,
both running and clumping. I'll let bamboo do the talk
when my American sisters come visit
my zen garden, treated with
serene whispers of kissing leaves and knocking canes
in a gentle wind.

Tonight I Hear the Crickets Sing: After Albert Goldbarth & Wang Wei

In the age of smartphones and sexbots, will poetry R.I.P.
in a digital coffin at the funeral of human language?
Enter Goldbarth's deliberate traditional, lyric bird, an irony
he creates for our era of big data and infobesity:
a scarlet brooch, on the velvet deep green breast of the forest.

Today AI can spit out 50 bird metaphors within seconds, even
though it has never touched velvet, tasted a dome of breast, or
breathed in a forest. Aren't we jealous of pre-CyberAge poets
who boast a readership less tech-bloated, less time-poor
and more word-hungry; who can carve lyrics about birds,
covets Goldbarth,
without self-consciousness, without irony,
once upon a time when there was time.
And then I hear the crickets. Wang Wei's crickets.
In the second couplet of a poem about getting old:
雨中山果落，　灯下草虫鸣。
Mountain fruits fall in the rain; field crickets sing in lamplight.

In 10 Chinese characters, this ink-thrifty poet slows us down
by showing:
when (autumn night: *fruits fall, lamplight*);
where (*mountain*, probably a cabin with *lamplight*);
who (Wang Wei);
what (*fruits fall, crickets sing*);
weather (*rain*, probably windy);
and most important, the why—
why would he/I/you/we care about poetry, birds, falling fruits, or
singing crickets after all?

Jiang Pu

Wang Wei (701?-761?) lived in the Tang Dynasty, so

those crickets have been chirping for over a millennium.

Question marks aside, we don't need to know

when exactly he was born or died. What matters

is that tonight, those crickets are still singing,

slow but steady, pacifying

the neon noise of digital tsunamis.

What matters is that Wang Wei heard the transient-eternal duet

of death and life in the tantric dance

of falling fruits and singing crickets;

and my human ears—which AI does not and will not have—

also hear their ensemble, even though they've rotten into soil that

has birthed new fruits for the birds that

have stirred poems such as Goldbarth's that

ripple a cosmic wave between me and you, my dear reader.

Citations are from Albert Goldbarth's poem *"Rhapsody at the End of Human Language"*
and Wang Wei's poem *"Autumn Night Sitting Alone"* (translated by Jiang Pu).

Dearest Floodplain Mother

Poetry Collection

Hasanah Mishahal Mansour

Hasanah Mishahal Mansour

Dearest Floodplain Mother,

I. Soil

Soil is tender upon the soles when pulverized.
        Soft when macerated, a woman's body.
Woman is I—women is we.
When woman was still a little girl,
        hands barely eight purpled the soap in my skin.
        The skin was made of clay, mind you!
Irony to the bleached, hourglass body the soap contoured.
        White. Safeguard branded.
Lilly Collins appeared on the old, beaten battered Samsung.
        Last night, supple—snow pale amidst
        pearl purl, sibilant hisses of the old Samsung.
She played Snow White.
        For Filipinos, whether moonful—moonless,
        nightly, daily is movie night; soap operas & so is karaoke.
Birthing the 11 a.m. thoughts, woman purpled our sallow skin
        with said soap once more.
"Caucasian wannabe," Brain said.
I wish I was still that little girl.

And whence the bourbon flush was drained from my skin
        replaced by a roseate blush—twelve:
        double zeros of that same day.
        I buried bone-deep, a toe that splayed holes on the [barely]
        breathing flesh-work of mother.
Cuspid tore the throat and in its jugular veins,
        spilled the, as ancestry said, "people of the flood pains."
        Maguindanaon. *Magi'ingeg*—people. *Danao*—lake.
I am engulfed in daydream.

II. Magui

"Magui," a friend once said. "It's not giving Magui."
    That time, November temper thawed;
    knees ire in crescent moons.
    Oh, word! Eccentric and odd was I thought.
The word familiar, barely edible.

Click. Clack.
Magui's tongue sucked its roof. Palate engulfing
    the whiff of flavored broth—livestock & noodles
    mingled in acrid organ, the J-shaped variety.
Magui sounded an awful lot like Maggi noodles.
We picked at our scabs as often as we spewed [non]existent slang.
    Such is *lodi*—idol. *Werpa*—power. If nonsense had its own,
    sensenun would be it.
In return, we also birthed five feet babes as often as we cut
    words five sizes small. Maguindanaon into *Magui*.

November sun ajar, shapened ado—akin ma's China.
    Notre Dame Fest's cultural espionage,
    a college competition.
At eighteen summers old, I retained
    a strange fondness for 'cultural dance'—a *legit* verbatim.
Perched atop four-legged plane, thighs spasming,
    spine mishappened, fingers arched obtusely
    & still—feet delicately poised.

Those who remained, taught their temples how to knit
    a rainbow, a subtlety for distaste.
    They had a difficulty maintaining said posey; but not I.
Magui's chin upturned. Pride is its analogy—a Magui's trait.
    Whereas, my lashes downturned—
    seduced by mother's beige.

It is a piece of me as I to it. Sallow skin, a testament
of old folks' vein wrung on woman's neck.

Eyes barely strewn shut, the dawn of rivalry entranced. *Inaul*—
    handwoven tubular skirts sported women's middle.
  Aureate bangles; hefty. Copious, kissed are those women palms
     whose ears benign in cold. Gold remained a staple
  in dances. A symbolism for a [half] dead lineage
  of royalty—whose children they bore developed a
  semblance of entitlement.
Gents strapped with bamboos opened the scene and
    a princess in tow atop said verdant beams.
    Likened, a nuptial feast
    ceased the scene, a *guinakit*—boat ate up
    space six feet between. Laden, in vibrant hues.
Silken red, blue, green, and yellow too!

III. There

There is a need for confrontation as the gaiety dwindles
    when all else departs & all that's left is exhaustion,
    home is a lone pavement in shambles.
Woman's forehead pecked the withered dorsum of Ma's hand.
    Ripe of decay & calloused of labor—fermented
    by detergent, a yesterday's forgotten page.

Rice is a Filipino's lifeblood ingested with supplementary carbs.
    And if poverty follows you, nary a flesh you will get.
Salt will be your only friend.
    Soy sauce, if likely—how blessed you'd be!
    I performed surgery on the cadaver of a fish.
I do not think; woman does not pause, I only gnawed carefully.

Tongue squirming—its mandibles attempt to wound me.

I do not let it.

Anon. The spoon's facet protruded an elongated reflection.

Whimsy. Eyes, two sizes smaller.

Lopsided features. "Am I pretty enough?"

Ma, parallel to mine—

recalled old wives' tale like a recurring ritual.

I'll be like her when I let tomorrow grow on me.

Do not trim your nails at night or you'll risk losing a loved one / hiccups make you taller / & so does jumping on New Year's Eve, twelve on the dot / but do not skip on your sister lest she sprouts miniscule, then insecure / lest you want to marry a widower, borne not your serenade as you cook / but wear that crimson garment on your exams, *"do not ask why, just do"* / cease whistling at twilight's peak, you'll invite all the *aswangs* unnoticeably / this is how you grow a debt of heart—you give twice what you have acquired / do not fasten the lid of a pot if a ladle bothers to peep / this is how you knock on wood when you invite misfortune on your tongue / take your *siestas* in the afternoon, child / & touch not your food till the family is all sat / this is how you eat the Filipino way / barehanded / you shape it like a beak / *"no, not like that!"* / Use the thumb to push it down / *"Yes"* / this is how your food trots off if you fail to scarf it down your throat / this is how to have a heart / this is how you get rid of pimples / extract the blood from your menses / paint your face red / twice, for good measure / *"give me a letter, I bit my tongue."* / Alas, this is how to have a come-whatmay mentality—sob your eyes & que sera you sing / don't be late at all / be very late / be late for five / be late for fifteen / be late for thirty / be late an hour / or don't show up at all / but what if I don't / & what if you do? / we're Filipinos, we have Filipino time.

I lied. I have long blurred the lines between
     what's not and what's there.
     I am becoming my Ma.
I am my mother's child through and through.

IV. Flood

Flood had long been woman's acquainted consort.
     Both betrothed as a child. Plaiting its glossy buttons
     on old Notre Dame pleats—sojourned of fate.
I grew up, flood besotted of me. Followed me.
     Be rid of me. Woman is called Magui for a reason.
     It is only right if flood swallowed me whole.
Just as it swallowed withered pieces of olden decay.

If I told you I was poor, you would deem me a liar.
     "Poor, are you now?" As I thought. I doubted not.
     "Is being poor a cultural thing?" I was shut. Tight-lipped.
     sewn and bothered. What am I supposed to say to that?
I left it—gently. Woman did not know how [not] to be gentle.
Dearest floodplain mother,
     I wish you ceased birthing gaunt babes and betrothing
     them to flood. We have plowed your remains,
     sowed in your stead.
Fished livestock to kiss them wholly.
     All in your command.

Herewith,
     If you're borne a slave; you'd die a slave.
     Scarcely is a chronicle embossed otherwise.

Ontology
of Water Memory

Poetry Collection

Elina Kumra

Elina Kumra

I.

In my dreams, tsunami is a woman with hair like kelp that swallows cities. 바다의 여자. Woman of the sea. She carries a salty perfume, speaks with a tongue that dissolves concrete. How to name what cannot be contained?

Call her 물의 기억, water memory. Call her the scalded splash of tea jarred from the cup I broke when the earth began to shake. I was boiling barley for dinner, watching the news. Now all news is the same news. Call her the blood-soaked shirt, rising biohazard.

If I speak her name, will she remember who I was before?

II.

The scientists measure in microsieverts, millirems, half-lives. I measure in empty shoes lined up outside the evacuation center. In the sudden absence of birdsong.

My mother says: our ancestors have seen worse. Before Fukushima, Nagasaki. Before that, war, famine, occupation.

I don't tell her that when I brush my hair, it falls out in clumps like wet seaweed. That I've started collecting it in jars labeled with dates, my own private data point. Some archives are kept in silence.

III.

Before tsunami, I was a woman who loved her morning cup of barley tea, who complained about train delays. After tsunami, I became a word in a foreign newspaper. Survivor. Evacuee. Data.

There's nothing poetic about disaster. No metaphor adequate for the smell of rotting fish on a shoreline, for the half-life of cesium in the soil where my grandmother once grew persimmons, sweet enough to make you cry. 남은 사람 – the ones who remain – carry water memory in our bones.

IV.

물의 여자 / woman of water

In Toba City, I trained as an ama diver, learned to hold my breath for three minutes, surfacing with a whistling gasp the tourists loved to photograph. "Japanese mermaid," they called me. Now I am old, but I still know the seabed better than the geography of my husband's weathered face.
When the wave came, I did not run.
I faced the rising wall of water, took one deep breath,
and dove back into the sea.
Did I choose to become part of her, or did she choose me?
Some transformations require no explanation.

V.

What blooms in irradiated soil:
dandelions with triple heads
white-feathered swallows
children who collect bottle caps instead of playing hide-and-seek
a new language of abbreviations (TEPCO, PBq, mSv/h)
wild boars with cesium-bright eyes
silence where there should be cicadas
my constant thirst

The white boar came to me in a dream, asked if I would trade my human tongue for one that could speak the grammar of ash. I woke with the taste of metal in my mouth.

VI.

After evacuation, the old people stopped eating. My grandmother set oranges on the altar beside my parents' photographs. The fruit remained perfect for months, as if even decay had abandoned us.

At night I searched for Fukushima on the internet. Found instead:
—American teenagers dressing as "radiation victims" for Halloween
—tour companies offering "disaster tourism" packages
—a porn star posing in a torn hazmat suit

I closed my laptop. Measured my pulse against the ticking of the Geiger counter the government installed in our temporary housing.
There's no poetic way to say: I am afraid, all the time.

VII.

When elephants kneel, pressing trunks to the ground like seismic antennae—

When cats slip through windows with whiskers fizzing like sparklers—
When snakes unscrew from hibernation, their bodies writing warnings in snow—

I should have known. The animals always know first.

At the evacuation center, I met a man they called "Radioactive Man," highest radiation levels ever recorded in a human. He cared for abandoned animals in the exclusion zone. Said he could see his future in their sickness.

"Sometimes I think of visiting my children in Tokyo," he told me, "but then I remember the dust in my clothes, my hair, my skin."

Some separations cannot be measured in kilometers.

VIII.

My daughter asks why she can't drink milk from the local cows.
Why we can't return to our house?
Why grandmother's hair has all fallen out?

I tell her about kintsukuroi[1], how broken bowls are mended with gold, becoming more beautiful for having been broken. Her small fingers trace the invisible fracture lines on my face.

"Are we broken?" she asks.

What is the weight of silence? How many becquerels in a half-truth?

IX.

In the dream, I am both water and what water destroys. Both the wave and the woman watching the wave approach. Both the broken vessel and the gold that fills its cracks.

어머니 says disaster is inherited like eye color, like the shape of hands, like the way we fold paper cranes for the dead.

Water has no memory, yet remembers everything. Holds it in its body like I hold my daughter's questions.

If I opened my mouth now, what would pour out? Salt or radiation? History or prophecy?

What name would you give to a woman who has swallowed the sea?

---

[1] Kintsukuroi (金繕い): "golden repair," the Japanese art of mending broken pottery with lacquer dusted with gold, treating breakage and repair as part of the object's history rather than something to disguise.

Swirlings

Poetry Collection

Anton Imbong

Anton Imbong

Swirlings One

It is only the most difficult days,
      when mornings feel like resurrection,
to spend a lifetime in the afternoon.
only for you to die in bed at night
without flowers,
the human person cannot fall asleep fast enough
      before the sun rises again.

      Here is the morning.
The birds are singing and the wind still has her voice.
      For me,
      this is swirling.
A whirlpool in the middle of the West Philippine Sea.
An invisible tornado between Katipunan and land bridges.
      Your expression when a man you used to know
      sits by the emergency exit.

      Everything stops.

Everything goes, death is a facial expression, a dream into abyss
      and abyss
      and sleep.

Swirlings Two

Towels hung over
Mattresses and pillow cases.
Humidity is a climate.
A language the human body speaks fluently—silently…

The temperature code switches,
From north to
south,
To windows, indigo.
It rings to keep warm,   the heart.
Lest it run out of our blood.

Winter here is rain
          and   hail.
Fluorescent concrete.
          Sketching   a   geometry   across   the   sky.
One could graph calamity with   ignorance.
One could graph the afterlife,
With chalk tied under
rubber boots.

As children jump, scraping their tired feet on recycled asphalt.

Humidity is a climate.
It is the *English* taught in our textbooks.
It is the typhoon that leaves you homeless.
It is a third language.

Imagined.

Anton Imbong

Swirlings Three

The crucifix

along Julia

Vargas, Stands at the crossroads. Until

the air is reduced to none. The savior has

left the cross.

To the footprints

of the lame

And wicked under

the light of

glass and steel.

It is not often you believe in poetry more than god.
It is not often that we drink the wine before the bread.

Casually

The architect leaves just enough rubble.
For the aesthetic of a promise.
Dropped on shelved grass.
Concrete linings make up our churches.

The wind.
She shifts   and   teeters.
Like buildings on shorelines,
Like your mother's back under lamplight.
She asks only for your grace.
As the savior steps down from the cross
Kneading skin, as bread is to wine.

Last Train Home

Poetry Collection

Jocelyn A. Chin

Jocelyn A. Chin

Shuiyang Forest

An earthquake pulls
new mountains from
this island's broken side.
A river is dammed.
A new lake is born
over a forest of cedar.
I am denuded.
I hope I am washed over
again and again
in this mineraled flow
till I am no longer myself,
but petrified, made strong.

Pedigree

grandpa had three fig trees in texas. two were yellow and one was purple. my aunt says they were the best figs she's ever eaten in her life, and that they were his real children. they would visit and he would ask do you want to see my figs? they were always sweet and perfectly plump and the juiciest figs she had ever tasted. they outshone the giant cucumbers and watermelon. all this in a small fenced-off backyard! we are all gone now but we drove past the house last week when we were in town. in the shadow of the evening we peered across the lawn and wondered if the trees still stood. all gardens are investments in the future. all things come apart and recombine. to send my aunt to the states before them, her parents gave her up. so she winds up in texas. my aunt, age twelve, was legally adopted by her own aunt, except she calls her her second mom. my grandparents later joined, stayed for twenty years, then moved up north, fighting and laughing and screwing up and sending down roots, hating the cold, then back to taiwan where the fruit is plentiful and sweet. she's still there. on a compost bin, someone has written: in nature there are no endings.

Jocelyn A. Chin

Last Train Home

The children play on the side of a road with a pile of jeans.

The babies nap on cutting boards among scrap cloths and shears.

The factories are on at night because everyone works overtime.

It's never over, it's just time.

The New Year has begun.

People wait at stations for seven straight days.

The operators are mad.

Nobody's ever making enough.

Every year, 130 million migrant workers leave farms for big cities.

Once every year, they try to go home.

The police in the crowd want to go home, too.

A woman with a giant pink bag wipes her face.

She pushes through the throng.

She could be fifteen.

The city empties but the city remains full.

A young boy pulls ears of corn with his grandma in a field.

He shucks the stalks with his red hands till they are bare.

The train cuts a harsh gray streak across the Guangzhou snow.

It slices on towards the circle of home.

The father loves his daughter to death, and she has no clue.

** Poem inspired by the 2009 documentary of the same title*

Mycelium

Poetry Collection

Anna Li Stollman

Anna Li Stollman

Mycelium

There are too many pocket dictionaries
on my bookshelf. New ones sprout
like a badly weeded garden; dry, spread thin
Which forgetting will I mourn the most?
I don't remember my mother tongue.
Too much alcohol in the vowels, too much fear
around the consonants.

Home was just a place to sleep. A crib-mate's
steady slumbered breathing. The heat rash
because the aunties couldn't fan us all at once.
Decency was a darkly formed dream that I drowned in.
The bridges here are different than the ones back home,
not enough ghosts haunting every crossroad.
Each morning, the hourglass spider
at the foot of my bed spins a new one.

The shower here is growing mold
around the edges, fuzzy and green and menacing.
There's only so much bleach can do, but
I am ruthless, Macbeth hunting Fleance,
out damned spore, out. I am tracing a question
in the condensation of the shower door. I am hoping
for ghost hands to write an answer back.
But what genesis can come from antiseptic?
There is no second beginning, diaspora set adrift
like the one I dream was stowed in my heart
to run aground here and colonize,
become new again.

I don't want Rome,
or a garden of peaches.
I want to walk and feel roots
against the soles of my feet.
I want to make suan la tang,
not Campbell's cream of mushroom.
I've never known the taste of my mother's cooking.

How many coincidences did it take for us to meet?
How much yuanfen, how many lives
of strangers brushing arms on the bus,
how many couples have stood
on the cracked asphalt beneath us
and looked at the same sunrise?
Maybe our ancestors dreamed
of us, our separate baby steps, the separate
journeys we would take to this godless country,
the way we twine together in the black ink
of night, like a red thread, respooled.

It would be arrogant to think we were the only ones
to see the view from here. Still, I can't
help feeling that we are, can't help wondering
about how much room for love we have
in this economy. It struck me
on the bridge of cobwebs, bent
over the railing like a hungry ghost as I watched
the way the day broke over the bay
and turned everything it touched to gold.

Anna Li Stollman

梅雨 (plum rain) / monsoon season

wet sidewalk leaves
becoming funeral
grounds, forests
of the dead
and damp
how much rot
has been buried here
how many graves
reinterred

monks chose with
preternatural care
where to pass
the rains
how long
they stayed a
mystery
undredged
oracle bones
in torrential
songs of
lives we cannot
remember
canyons that
carried water
once and might
again one day
calling clouds
down from
the heavens

asceticism is
for the dogs
long months
with only dew
or telegrammed
love for food
mudras
cannot shield us
from the rain
we are barefoot
in languid streets
overflowing storm
drains making eddies
hungry river mouths
around our feet

take me back to
discovering holes
in the sand
my fingernails
become pockets
of seashell bodies
my fingers
foreign bodies
a shriveled carcass
of clay

take me back
to the desert
these puddles are
no longer for me

Anna Li Stollman

东北摇篮曲 / Cradle Song for my Birth Mother

A name is a gift that can't be returned.
She gave me a new one, a borrowed
outfit that chafed at my shoulders.
I used to sit on my bed and fold it
so that it could be worn again the next day.
Where did you bury them, the ones
you never gave me? I imagine the womb
of an unmarked grave, unspooling into
damp earth. Receipts lost to wind, forgotten
blessings for a mountain god's temple
scratched in chalk, gone
with the next rain

I've learned to conjure
their noise, play at their
pronunciation. Oily syllables that
slip from my mouth like sand, dust
that gathers on a mantle.
Did you sing to me? The only
lullabies I know are wrong, but
the trees outside my window hum
to me each night and the sound—it hunts
through the earth for an echo

In the spring, I watch
the rivers flood. Are the hills here
like the ones back home?
I've heard it rarely snows there;
winter bruises my knees, fools me
into thinking I already know this
in the marrow of my bones.

Summer leaves me remembering
everything I had to teach myself,
old songs that don't sound
the same. I don't sleep anymore.
The moon is too dull and
the wind, not quiet enough.

Did you know? That day
at the airport? Did a
magpie fly to tell you
that I fell asleep on the plane,
and she marveled at
how still and quiet
I was.

Moribund

I've still never learned
how to catch a fish.
Flies, sure—with vinegar.
Mice and colds, plenty.
I can hold my own hand
and fold my own dumplings,
and I've never had to change
a tire for real, but if I had to,
I could,
goddammit.

The hole in your backyard
buried midden barren land.
Nothing grows here but
root channels spread

to soundless samsara depths.
Leave your offerings here,
a mother's cherished keepsakes,
everything you promised
to become, all that you
hope to carry along
after rebirth.

It's getting late.
How to begin again
in winter, season of
endings, how the sun
curls like pink ribbons
sweeping the clouds
and earth, like salt
that clings to your
lonesome trailing hems.

No amount of soy milk
or wool socks
in this world
in this life,
will keep you from
being spare and lonely
in the dark.

Gender

The Salted Fish Turns Over

Jade Mah-Vierling

Baisha Village, February 1924 - Age 17

Mei's heart thumped like fish trapped in a net as she dipped her hand into the salt pot. Remembrance of what she'd done, the deal she'd struck, made the tips of her ears grow warm. She needed to be quick. She needed to be precise.

With a fistful of coarse grains, Mei poured a line of salt the width of her smallest finger along the pounded earth threshold of the servants' quarters. Escaped grains danced away. She stretched to sweep them back into place.

She would be safe. For now.

Behind her, a watery morning sun spilled into the barren room, illuminating two bamboo sleeping mats, each with a neat pile of ragged blankets at its foot, and a once-beautiful chest of drawers. Rising, she faced the second of the two mats. Emotion clamoured for release, and her throat tightened. She swallowed the hard lump and stepped toward the window to line its narrow sill,inspecting the salt to ensure there were no gaps. She would need to check it every day to make sure the lines remained unbroken.

The room belonged solely to her. Her ancestors' servants were long gone, and with eight brothers, there were no other spaces to spare in their single-courtyard house. Since it was removed from the other sections of the dwelling, there was little chance of anyone seeing the salt. If it could protect her, she would have time to finish secondary school, move to the city, and become Baisha's first female teacher.

Mei expelled a sigh through her nose. Inside the pot, grains of salt glimmered back at her. With a tilt, its smooth bottom yawned, making her gut clench. She had used too much. Someone would notice when it came time to preserve their meats with salt and sunlight.

She exited the servants' quarters into chilly, damp air framed by an overcast sky, and crossed the courtyard to the heavy wooden doors. Inside, she cushioned each step with an exaggerated knee bend before arriving in the mercifully empty kitchen. She set the salt pot gently onto its shelf next to the other squat, clay pots. They were all nearly empty, just like everything else—bank accounts, patience, hope.

A rustle of fabric made Mei leap away from the shelf, stubbing a bare toe on the stone hearth. She cursed inwardly as her mother approached with a bundle of kindling. The skin between Li Jeng's brows was pulled tightly—a permanent expression.

"Why have you not fetched the water?" Her mother's tone was sharp as a fishhook, eyes discerning, as she studied her only daughter.

"I came to get the carrying pole."

"Well, hurry up. Baba and your brothers will be back for breakfast. Did you get no sleep? You look terrible."

June 1913 - Age 6

Typhoon rains pelted the roof of the servants' quarters, mingling with the crescendo of boar-like snores coming from Mei's eldest brother, Xiyang. If she hissed at him to be quiet, he would roll over, the snores evaporating only long enough for her to find sleep. With eyes fixed on the crumbling ceiling, she sucked in a breath and attempted to speak.

Her mouth stayed resolutely shut.

Fear flooded her stomach as she tried to lift an arm.

She couldn't move.

As a villager of Baisha, she knew what this was—an invisible spirit was pressing her down.

For hours, she endured the invisible force until her mind grew tired, joining her body in sleep.

By morning, the memory was not gone. She flexed her fingers to remind herself that she could, that she was in control.

It was bad luck to be visited by spirits in the night, but she would keep it to herself. She would bear the fear alone.

Today was a welcome distraction, a day that didn't always arrive for girls in her village. School. Although city girls were now attending school, such trends took longer to reach rural areas. In the village of Baisha, educating future brides was a waste.

With a stomach full of paddy eel and rice, Mei trundled along the dusty path to school. Her family was by no means rich, but they could operate their household without her. Most village children stayed home to help their fathers tend to the livestock and land, or their mothers to house and family.

As she passed the well, she spied Fēn, a girl her age who'd quit school after the sudden death of her sister. Fēn lowered a bucket into the well, flicking her wrist to tip and fill it once it reached the bottom.

Something tugged at Mei's vision as she passed.

It glinted next to Fēn's sandalled foot. A pearly white snake, its scales glistening in the sun, coiled next to Fēn's ankle.

"Fēn! Behind you!" cried Mei.

Lazily, the snake unfurled the tip of its pointed tail.

"There! At your feet!"

Fēn couldn't see it. Her face scrunched in confusion as she scoured the ground. "What do you see, Mei?" Fēn's limbs trembled with the effort of hauling up the leaden bucket that only became heavier as it neared the top.

Mei blinked hard.

The snake was gone. It was only Fēn and her too-large, hand-me-down sandals.

"I… I thought I saw something," she said, turning back to the path. Her cheeks burned.

All the way to school, she pondered the snake.

March 1924 - Age 17

With her doorway and windowsill salted, the nights passed by easily for the first time in months. Mei surrendered into sleep's open arms, her body depleted from caring for the household and its inhabitants, her mind ready to escape physical existence.

Mei hadn't always needed the salt.

She'd been six the first time a spirit had visited her in the night. It was her secret that it still happened once a year on a sweltering summer night when Xiyang's snoring was too loud, or the air too thick to breathe. She could stomach the inability to move or speak. Barely. But the last time, the spirit had shown itself. It would return for what she owed.

Mei was not going to let that happen.

Her mother had taught her which foods opened the channels of the body, allowing yin and yang to flow in harmony. Rejecting her mother's advice, she consumed heavy, oily foods to stagnate her qi. Fatty cuts of meat and overly-oiled vegetables made her stomach gurgle in protest, but she couldn't let her vitality strengthen the spirit.

By the second week of her new diet, Mei thought she saw a scaly white tail whip into a thicket of shrubs.

May 1924 - Age 17

A tinny knock echoed through the window to the main house. Mei's floured hands hovered above a stuffed dumpling she had been about to press closed.

The men were out in the fields.

The rap repeated.

Mei wiped her hands firmly on her apron and crept into the courtyard. "Who's there?"

"There's been an accident," called a young voice.

Heart thumping, Mei unfastened the door to reveal a boy no older than twelve, covered in grime from working the paddies.

"There's been an accident with the ox cart," he said, still out of breath. "Xiyang is hurt."

"Does he need the doctor?" Her heart kicked like an ensnared fish.

"The men sent me to fetch Dr. Zhang."

"Where is Xiyang?"

"In the ox paddock by the stables."

Mei bowed her head to the boy, who took off down the street.

She was not to leave the house save for school or fetching water. She left anyway. Her brother was easy to find. A group of onlookers had gathered around a slanted ox cart in the grassy paddock. Finding an opening, she forced herself through the men. Two scowled at her; scandalized by girls and women outside of the home.

Xiyang lay sprawled on his back, dazed eyes staring at the powder blue sky, sweaty bangs plastered to his forehead. One leg protruded at a strange angle, and he clutched his chest.

"Mui Mui," he said weakly. Despite his pained expression, his golden-brown eyes glowed a luminescent amber, like a candle flame through linen.

"What happened?" she asked.

"The ox got spooked by something… nearly jumped out of her skin. The cart lost a wheel… rammed into me."

"What spooked it?"

One of the men cut in. "It was a great white snake, biggest I've ever seen." Ice trickled through Mei. It was no accident. This was her doing from the bargain she'd selfishly struck.

"Dr. Zhang is coming," said Mei. She wanted to cradle her brother in her arms until he was well, but she suppressed the urge. The sight of sturdy Xiyang, his skin more tanned than hers from his hours in the fields, in such a compromised position, crushed her own heart beneath the weight of the cart.

"Move aside," commanded a stern voice. The village doctor was dressed like the others in loose-fitting fabrics, wearing the same overworked expression. He was highly sought after as the only doctor for miles. While most doctors checked body parts for warmth or coolness, the tongue for infections, and the pulse for weakness of heart, Dr. Zhang could see the meridians of the body.

The doctor stooped low, listening to Xiyang's recounting of events as he pressed various spots on his leg.

Xiyang responded with a deep groan.

The doctor pressed along his ribs.

Xiyang's protesting was quieter.

Dr. Zhang took scarcely a minute to complete his examination then stood and turned. His eyes fixed for a moment on Mei. Then he addressed the men.

"He can be moved home. Fetch a cart so his leg can lie flat. I will join you when I've collected the herbs." A few men left to retrieve the cart while the others pulled Xiyang into a seated position, his face a colourless moon.

Mei bowed her head in thanks to the doctor.

"I've often wondered how you became the most educated girl in Baisha," he said, observing her in a way that made her feel like one of his patients. Mei's cheeks warmed at his direct address. "Your family has a bā shé, does it not?"

"A bā shé?" Blood pounded in her ears and chest.

"Half spirit, half beast, they manifest as a great snake large enough to devour an elephant. They feed on human qi and convert it to magic. Many will grant wishes in exchange for such a connection to our world."

Despite the sun blazing high in the sky, a chill kissed Mei's spine. A question surfaced. "How do you get rid of a bā shé?"

"When it is not given what is promised, it will haunt its prey. Each night—when the veil between worlds thins—it siphons their qi, until there is nothing left."

"What if it has no qi to feed on?" Perhaps she could starve it.

"I caution you. The bā shé always takes what is owed."

June 1923 - Age 16

"Ma Ma, why have the girls left school?" Seated on their dusty front steps weaving worn strips of fabric into a rug, Mei and Li Jeng attempted to catch a non-existent breeze.

Mei's mother didn't look up. Her knuckles were rounded from overuse. "They have a duty to family."

"Can't their duties be fulfilled when they're older?"

"Duty does not wait."

"Why did Xiyang leave school?"

"Your brother knew his place. He knows what he must do to attract a worthy bride."

"I'll never be a bride," said Mei. She plucked a strand of teal fabric from their basket. The cloth came from an old shirt of hers.

"You have no choice. Your father says you are not going back to school when the fall comes."

The silk went slack in Mei's hands. "But Ma—"

"One day, you will understand," said Li Jeng.

"I do understand," pleaded Mei. "But it's not me. I'm not like—"

"You are exactly like the other girls in this village. The difference is they do not have a mother like me."

"How does that help me?" muttered Mei indignantly.

"You will respect your elders and what you are fortunate not to know."

Mei's head hung. Despair seeped through her bones, begging to spill onto the parched ground, wiping away everything in her sad, sorry village life. She pushed the emotion down, once again. She wove silent tears and vibrant strands into the rug, where they nestled with the grey and brown fabric.

That night, Mei didn't bother hissing at her brother to quit snoring. For hours, she stared unseeingly at the ceiling. An itch crept to her nose. She reached to scratch it.

Her hand didn't move.

She tried again with the other. Nothing.

The hairs on her arms rose abruptly. Squinting through moonlit darkness, she could see two corners. The first was empty. The second was not. Thick shadows writhed within it, growing.

She blinked hard, breathing in deeply to slow her frantic heart.

A spirit emerged from the corner. She was female, but ancient, otherworldly. Inky hair pooled at her bare feet and she wore a pearl-white dress that glimmered like milky snakeskin. There was a caged wildness about her.

Mei's scalp prickled. The other nights had merely been darkness and the excruciating inability to move. But as the spirit crouched beside her, Mei missed those nights.

It couldn't be real. It had to be a dream, a nightmare. It would pass.

The spirit peered into her face with orb-like eyes bristling with sharp lashes.

"Child, I heard you call out to me."

It took Mei a moment to realize the spirit's lips had not moved, nor had sound escaped them. The words were as clear inside her mind as if they had been uttered aloud.

"You're shrouded in misery. What ails you tonight?"

"What?!" thought Mei. Afraid that the spirit was in her head, Mei shifted the focus. She formed a thought. "Who are you?" she asked.

"I'm everything and I'm nothing, just as you are. The difference is that I am neither here nor there. I exist in the in-between. You Earthlings exist in the here."

"This isn't real," thought Mei. Her racing heart said differently.

"How would you like to become the most educated girl in your village?"

Mei couldn't help but imagine a life outside Baisha, where the air didn't reek of fish guts and salt.

"For a price of course," added the spirit.

June 1924 - Age 17

Mei shook with silent rage as she carried the tray of pungent *bai zhi* tea and steamed *fú líng* mushrooms out of the room Xiyang had inhabited during his recovery. His body had been taken away for burial.

Dishes clattered with each step, threatening to topple to the ground. Her beloved, hardworking brother had lived only a quarter moon's cycle until succumbing to his injuries. Having pressed the doctor for information on the herbs, Mei discovered that *bái zhǐ* tea and *fú líng* mushrooms had been prescribed to manage pain and induce calmness.

The doctor had known Xiyang would not live.

Mei's ears burned each time she thought of her brother's fate. It was her fault for making a bargain with the *bā shé*.

To receive, something had to be taken. Nature's balance.

☙

Plumes of steam billowed from the pot behind Li Jeng. "You would waste such a precious resource!"

Mei cowered before her mother.

Hair had fallen out of the usually-neat knot at the nape of her neck, framing ruddy skin pulled tight across bony features. "You would have our fish go bad for lack of salt! You would have us all starve, you stupid girl!"

Mei's head hung. She had taken salt each time the lines in her quarters had thinned.

"You have your education but still no sense! Your father changed his mind. He let you go to school in the hopes that your desire for freedom would abate, that you would learn your place in the world. It has done nothing but put silly ideas in your head about dieting and talking with spirits."

Heat throbbed in Mei's ears and cheeks. Her eyes fixed on the hem of her mother's skirt. A loose thread dangled precariously.

"Look at me, girl."

Mei raised her eyes to meet her mother's and pain erupted through her cheek as a palm connected with it. Pinpricks of light burst in front of her. Mei collapsed to the ground, her cheek pulsing as she hit the stone floor. Traitorous tears escaped.

"You will not leave this house until I find someone willing to take you as their bride. Out of my kitchen!" The pot behind Li Jeng wailed and belched smoke.

Mei stumbled across the courtyard into the quarters she'd once shared with her brother. The doorway and windowsill had been wiped clean. Months of hurt poured out of Mei as she collapsed onto Xiyang's mat. She sobbed until the pressure lessened, a raging river becoming a gentle stream. Blinking swollen eyes, Mei stared at the exposed doorway.

She wasn't safe.

She wondered what would happen if she evaded sleep all night. Would the bā shé still come for her? Mei sat up, cross-legged, intending to remain so all night.

Three hours after midnight, Mei slumped against the wall, having finally relinquished wakefulness. A dense silence filled the room, shadows thickening in corners.

Mei ran through a field of wildflowers. She could do whatever she wanted, go anywhere, be anyone. The ground pitched her sideways. Legs collapsed beneath her as she tumbled and spun. Colour drained from the field until nothing but darkness remained, her stomach filled with a dizzying weightlessness.

When she awoke, Mei's spine was round and sore. She attempted to push herself fully upright.

She couldn't move.

As she had done a year before, the bā shé glided out of the shadows. Her movements were fluid, no—serpent-like. She stopped at the edge of the mat. Her large eyes didn't match the dimensions of her other features.

The hairs on Mei's arms stood.

"There you are, Mei Chin," said the bā shé into Mei's mind. "For a year in your service, a tragedy befell you."

"Why did you have to take him?"

"Sorrow lasts the longest; you humans never let it go."

Mei desperately tried to move her body. Her limbs would not obey.

"Clever of you to block your qi and protect yourself with salt. I will still receive what is owed, no matter how long it takes. Even if there is nothing left of you. Magic requires sustenance. I did an awful lot of magic for you, changing your father's mind about school. How unappreciative you are," drawled the bā shé.

"You did nothing for me! My mother spoke with him."

"Ha! You think your mother has that kind of influence. You know what you are? Like every other villager, you're greedy. You think you're different, but you're not."

"I want to live a good life."

"You have more than what most have in this village and yet you long for the salted fish to turn over."

The bā shé floated toward Mei, her skin dull, hair tattered and unkempt. Her eyes glinted as she crouched, her nose close enough to touch Mei's.

Acrid breath was unnaturally sweet in Mei's nostrils. She had smelled that scent before.

A lost memory flickered out of reach: a blur of darkness and light. Distorted. Like looking through the surface of water. She hoped the bā shé had not seen it. She focused on the image, reeling it toward her like a stubborn fish. Her head ached with the effort until finally… it slipped into her conscious mind. It was like remembering something she'd always known.

The bā shé had visited her many times, standing over Mei's paralyzed form then hiding the memory when a bargain was not struck. Bound by ancient magic, the bā shé could only bargain with an individual on the longest night of the year. Desperate for sustenance in a village that was becoming more educated, the bā shé had left Mei with a partial memory of their last encounter.

Mei pressed a thought toward the bā shé: "I never made a deal with you. I have always denied you. Everyone in this household has denied you."

Was that true? Her stomach clenched. Her mother had said salt wouldn't protect her. When Mei had last seen her mother, Li Jeng's cheeks were sallow, her eye sockets deep. Had her mother made a bargain?

Heat grew behind Mei's eyes as tears slid down cheeks she could not wipe.

The bā shé's face contorted, her otherworldly beauty vanishing, features skeletal and severe. A face Mei had seen before.

"You lie!" hissed the bā shé.

"You made a deal with my mother, not me."

The bā shé's eyes bulged. "Are we not clever from attending school—with my help, no less."

"You have been compensated, have you not? You took my brother's life as payment. We owe you nothing!"

"Are you not curious about your mother's wish?" said the bā shé with a wicked grin. "I'll tell you. She's been nourishing me in exchange for your education. Most women in this village make deals for their sons to marry prosperously. Yours exchanged your education for your brother's life!"

"That's not true."

"You're right again. She didn't know what I would take from her. That is how desperate she was for you to escape your womanly fate. Your dear mother has been on your side this whole time! I took your brother's life potential and gave it to you."

"No." Mei's thought was edged with doubt.

"How painful to have scorned your mother and stolen your brother's future!"

Mei wanted to press her hands into fists but found her limbs as immovable as stone.

"Our debt is paid," said Mei. "Leave and never return!"

"Is that your wish?" asked the bā shé, a sly smile appearing.

"No. It's a command. If our deal is complete, you must leave this house and all of its inhabitants!"

The bā shé's nostrils flared, her eyes widening. "You will not command me!" she shrieked into Mei's mind. The sound rattled her like silver coins in a jar. As if the bā shé had no power to refuse a direct order, a force dragged her backwards toward the shadowy corner. She attempted to step forward again but each time she raised a dirty sole, she was yanked backwards, as if by a collar. Clutching at her neck, the bā shé struggled once more before she was sucked into darkness.

Mei sat, frozen in awe, until she realized she could once again move.

Calgary, Canada, 2001

The girl beside Mei was small for her size; she had to sit on her knees to see into her bowl. The girl wielded chopsticks expertly—not a single fleck of sauce tarnished the white tablecloth.

"I have something for you," said Mei to her great-granddaughter.

The girl looked into Mei's worn face and put down her chopsticks.

Mei pressed a smooth, red envelope with gold characters into her outstretched palms.

"Thank you, Bak Bak," she said, but Mei's arthritic fingers hadn't let go.

"This is for university," said Mei.

"But I'm in grade one."

Staring into those eyes made Mei's breath catch in her throat. The girl watched with the golden eyes of the brother Mei had lost so many years ago.

"I want you to save it for university. If you drop out and get married instead, you have to pay me back."

"Yes, Bak Bak," said the girl.

"Give it to your mother for safe keeping."

The girl handed the fat envelope to her mother, who slid it into her purse without a glance.

Mei and her great-granddaughter turned back to their bowls.

The women who had come before her, and those who would come after, were present in Mei's mind as she bit into steamed *xián yú*— salted fish.

For My Mother
Who Learned to Smile in a Foreign Language

Poetry Collection

Vaswati Das

Vaswati Das

For My Mother, Who Learned to Smile in a Foreign Language

My mother wears her trauma like a second sari,
drapes it over her shoulders every morning, muscle memory—
the way a child-bride learns to walk without making a sound,
the way a daughter learns to watch her mother disappear.

In my dreams, I'm always eight years old, watching her pick up
the pieces of her shattered bangles after my father's fists. I'd say,
"Maa, one day we'll have a house so big
your voice won't echo when you weep. One day
I'll build you a home where no man can reach you."

Now we have marble floors that gleam like fresh milk,
but my mother still walks like she's crossing a minefield.
Her *mangalsutra* hangs between her breasts like a grenade,
tick tick ticking with every heartbeat.

Did you know that a mother's silence can become
her daughter's entire language? That grief has a taste
like *kerela* bitter on the tongue, that it passes
from mother to daughter like a cursed diamond?

At night, I catch my reflection wearing her face,
her eyes rimmed with *kajal* and all the words
she never said. In this land, we're both foreigners—
her accent thick as ghee, mine bleached SoBo clean.

Don't tell me healing comes with time.
Time is just more space for haunting.
My mother's ghosts have moved into my body,
made a temple of my ribcage, turned my heart
into their prayer room.

Every time I open my mouth to speak,
her silences fall out like broken teeth.

My Mother's Ghost

In the kitchen where
my mother's ghost kneads *aata*
    her hands translucent
    as mosquito nets in the humid Bengal light
    she is unmade—
    a negative space between *ruti* and remembering
    her fingers ghost-folding memories into dough

    What survives: the scent of cardamom and unspoken violence
        dowry ledgers etched into her soft palms
        saris pressed with the weight of centuries
        each fold, a language of survival

Here, daughters are born calculating:
    the mathematics of arranged marriages
    the geometry of acceptable grief
    the quantum mechanics of silence

Listen: how the monsoon carries her whispers
    through coconut groves and abandoned marriage contracts
    how her ghost walks the thin line between
    devotion and self-immolation

Trigger warning: in this landscape
    survival is a womanly dialect
    a language of sideways glances
    of measured breaths
        of silence disguised as submission

She haunts me in Bangla and English
    code-switching between oppression and possibility a spectral
    translation of what cannot be said
    what will never be said

Vaswati Das

Lessons in Translucence, for Little Girls

In the kitchen's fluorescent glare, my *dida*
performs her daily ritual of diminishment—
each gesture precise as prayer,
each breath, a careful subtraction
from the sum of her presence.

I catalog her disappearing:
spine curved like the Barak at dusk,
footsteps whispering against earthen floor
softer than dust settling on brass vessels,
softer still than memory's unraveling thread.

While men's voices ricochet off walls
she dissolves into steam,
into the negative space between
counter and cupboard, word and silence,
into the geometry of absence.

My aunt studies this alchemy,
this inheritance passed down like wedding gold:
how to fold your hunger small enough
to nest between your molars,
how to turn your breath to morning mist,
your bones to frost on window glass.

At ten, I was all sharp edges and questions,
my voice, a stone thrown into still water.
Why? I demanded of her silence.
Why? Of her shoulders' quiet slope.
The *daal* simmered, yellow as autumn light,
while outside, men's voices swelled,
inconsiderate thunder I longed to become.

There are sins of survival
and sins of privilege—
the latter gilded in self-absolution,
wrapped in the silk of assumed right.
I learned this watching her hands
perform their tender violence
of self-erasure.

My mother had forged me differently—
hammered my voice into steel,
bade me to cast shadows
longer than my body.
I would take up space like revenge, she said,
like farmers burning vast stores of indigo,
while my grandmother's hands performed
their familiar dance of disappearing.

Sometimes she would watch me
across the dinner table,
her eyes wide as empty plates,
as if I were some strange new species
she had never dreamed could bloom
from her own translucent bone.

Art of a Courtesan

Lucy Zhang

The nine-tailed fox eats deflowered courtesans. The women who act sly during their checkers matches, tea ceremonies, and fan dances. These courtesans disappear from the brothels, disgraced and in debt, without their virginity that could've been bought out for a fortune—the kind of fortune that elevates you to another economic class. The nine-tailed fox drags these women to the mountain of Qingqiu overnight, leaving a path of fallen hair and fur in its wake.

My mother was eaten by the nine-tailed fox shortly after she birthed me, leaving me in the care of the brothel, saddled with her debt to the manager who'd clothed her in the finest dresses and paid for her lessons in etiquette and crafts. The debt has only tripled since then to account for the money spent raising me as a baby to a helper servant to a courtesan-in-training. Despite the promotion in my title, I still bury the day's fresh dung and dig new holes for the next day, light incense by the bathrooms so the scent doesn't overtake you, wash sweat and sex-scented linens that have slowly lost their color due to the bleaching effect of vaginal discharge. The closest I've come to providing entertainment is delivering and replenishing tea to tables while guests play card games or flirt with their paired courtesan.

"If only you had a body half as good as your face," the manager often laments. I am too scrawny for the men who visit. My mother was thin too, but she wore her thinness like a swan, while I wear it like a sickly fawn.

Sometimes, I think of running away to Mount Qingqiu in search of my mother. I refuse to believe the nine-tailed fox ate her. My mother was too beautiful to die like that—even death would hesitate in the wake of her closed eyes and quieting breaths. But the days are too busy, and my dreams of packing a sack of bao and stealing into the night vanish as quickly as the evening candle loses fuel. I'd rather leave debt-free, so no one can lord the value of opening my legs over me. The manager says that if I work hard, I might even be able to leave without selling my virginity, although I think she's just saying that to get me to clean out the toilets. Even the most beautiful courtesans are far from a state of financial independence.

The first time I meet my father (though I wouldn't know he was my father until later), the manager calls me over to help prepare a plate of jasmine cookies and refined Anhua black tea. We rarely use this tea because of the price, and instead, the supply sits at the back of our storage closets, loosely pressed in uniform black bricks. I slam a knife down on the brick, severing a cluster of leaves to brew. I hope the brewing process resembles our standard green tea enough, where just a small handful creates a strong fragrance.

My father wears a long, black robe patterned with red silk on the sleeves and neckline, the fabric shining with any small movement under light. His long hair is pulled tightly away from his face, not a strand falling free to frame his cheekbones or cover his pointed, large ears. I pour tea as he and the manager chat. I've learned to tune conversations out and focus on my duties, a skill useful when higher-up officials drink their cheeks red and begin to spill secrets. More stories of corruption and slow, year-long poisonings flow through the brothel than you'd think, and it's best not to fixate or else you might end up caught in the fray, the execution of a disposable servant girl as collateral damage. But as dumb a servant as I try to be, it's hard to ignore the manager's crackling, sharp voice, one I've been trained to react to even while asleep.

"We don't take commissions to find the remains of courtesans," the manager says, tone curt, as though she'd rather be cleaning the toilets than deal with the man across from her. She taps her nails on the table. "No matter how much money you put on the table. If you were truly serious, you'd have stopped by years ago, while she was still here, swollen with your spawn."

My father claims he was busy with work. Something to do with the war and other political terminology I don't fully understand. He offers to buy out all the lower-tier courtesans who can rarely pay back the manager's investments—food, clothing, shelter, education in the arts and entertainment. Most of the girls end up as financial losses, but the ones who shine through like diamonds make enough profit for the rest of the brothel to live comfortably. Diamonds like my mother.

The manager pinches her brow and blinks slowly, a sign of simmering fury. "You realize you ruined the courtesan you're searching for, right? It's a dead-end task. You had your night of passion, and now you've got to live with the consequences. We don't produce courtesans like her every other day, you know."

I stand to the side after pouring tea, watching closely when the liquid in their cups dwindles.

"I'll buy out your servants," he offers before grabbing my wrist.

The manager erupts into laughter. "I suppose I shouldn't be surprised you can't even recognize your own spawn if they're not decorated in rouge and low-cut cheongsams."

My father turns toward my face and pulls me closer. His expression shifts from tight and guarded to something more pensive—not quite gentle, but not agitated either. His eyes shift across my face and he pulls away the baby hair in front of my eyes. His gaze drifts down my body, lines concealed by rippling silk too large for my frame—the shedded skins of the older girls, so we liked to call the hand-me-down gowns they left us. He turns toward the manager without releasing his grip. I eye the empty teacup in the manager's wrinkly hands.

"I take that back," he says. "I don't need to find her body. I'll buy this one back instead. How much?"

"Back?" The manager repeats, eyes narrowing. "There's no *back*. My staff lose their pasts the moment they enter this place."

My father releases his grip on me, and my arms instinctively move toward the teapot to fill the empty cups. The manager swats my arm. "You're going to give this old woman kidney failure from all this tea. Tell the others to prepare dumplings. With meat. Don't water them down with chives and cabbage this time."

I bow, leaving the tea set, and head to the back kitchen, where the girls who aren't pretty enough to serve work. As I retreat, I hear the manager curse, "You men are always such fools. Empty your clogged eardrums and listen clearly: there is *nothing* you can buy here anymore. We don't accept customers like you."

"I'll return," my father replies. "I hope you reconsider the offer and the future of your girls."

I don't catch the manager's response. I've already arrived at the kitchen, where chopped scallions catch a flick of oil, sizzles erupting in waves, and steam whispers from between woven bamboo strips that hold hot bao and slippery rice noodle rolls.

"The boss wants denser dumplings," I holler over the sounds. "Less vegetables. More pork." The girl closest to me responds with a curt nod. Only one person needs to hear—the kitchen girls operate like a team of ants, constantly in sync to deliver on a mission. I return to the courtesan's quarters to help the popular beauties with their makeup and clothing, a standard routine when the brothel isn't too busy and I too am enlisted in serving lower paying customers with beverages.

"Thank goodness Mei is here," Elder Sister Jade says as I step into a room descending into chaos, clothing strewn on the floor and piled over each other, makeup smeared over some of the courtesans' lips. Elder Sister Jade's eye shadow is so blotched her eyes look more like mangosteens sunk into her sockets.

"We could've avoided this whole situation if you'd simply left the politician with me instead of leading him into your bed," Elder Sister Pearl sighs. The top courtesans are named after precious stones and gems. When you reach such high ranks, you lose your old identity completely to maintain a mask of intrigue for customers.

"Customers don't like real people, they come here to escape," the manager always says. But I think the real reason is that most girls would rather fashion a new identity than carry on their names given by those who'd abandoned them. Pearl, despite her origins from a wealthy merchant family, had been left behind at the brothel after her birth since she was the fourth girl, and their family had been hoping for a boy.

"What happened?" I ask as I begin to pick up the dresses on the floor.

"A particularly daring customer decided he could have an orgy with a whole party of us because Jade here thought it'd be a brilliant idea to take him to one of the private rooms," Pearl begins.

"That's only because you were boring him with your repetitive elephant chess games. No customer likes to lose every. Single. Time," Jade rolls her eyes. "Mei, could you fix my eyes? No need to deal with the dresses. They were old anyway. We'll be getting replacements."

I leave the pile of discarded dresses on a shelf so no one will trip over the sleeves or get hooked on the sequins. Then I twist open a jar of powdered rice and dab over Jade's blotchy cheeks and delicate eyelids, like a fresh fall of snow fading human features into an angel's. Despite her attitude and wit, Jade wields her features like a child, innocent and lovely and deceptively unaware of when her robes dip and the skin below her neckline catches the breeze. That's why I prefer to keep her makeup clean, outlining her eyes with thin black lines of Dai, coloring her cheeks with my fingers dipped in light shades of rouge. No Huadian dottings or blood-red eye shadow. Jade stays quiet as I dab at her lips with oil, adding back signs of life to the dry, wrinkled skin. She eats too many salty foods and never drinks enough water despite the manager's nagging, and the rest of us are complicit in sneaking Jade lamb skewers because we feel bad that she can't enjoy what she loves best: sodium. I suppose willingly leaving your family for full meals will do that to you. I'm not certain Jade's family is still alive, but none of us dare to ask, especially after all Jade's stories about eating crickets and gnawing on corn stalks.

"Thanks Mei, you're a dear," Jade says after I've finished. I dust my hands on my skirts and proceed to the lineup of courtesans waiting for their makeup to be redone, even the ones with small lip smudges who could wipe it up themselves. I roll up my sleeves until they bunch in thick layers above my elbows and stretch my arms over my head. Then I ready my supplies, each girl a different color scheme and aesthetic, like wildflowers left to grow freely.

⁶ꝫ

As I prepare to sleep and wipe off the little remaining powder on my face, the manager calls me to her office.

"Listen here," she whispers. "You need to leave tonight. I've packed you a bag of food, clothing, and money—enough for you to get by for a few days. Follow the road until where it meets the horizon, and then make a left toward the mountains. You can get to Qingqiu Mountains that way." She pushes a heavy sack into my arms.

"I need to leave?" I ask. I never planned to stay forever, but I hadn't even paid off my debts.

"*That* man is going to come for you tomorrow. He'll take you by force if needed, and we only have so much power against the imperial fools."

"Did he not offer enough money? Is that why I need to go?"

The manager pats my head. "Silly girl, no amount of money in the world can protect you from a man like that. You're better off seeking help from the nine-tailed fox who should owe you protection at minimum, given the price your mother paid." She shoos me out the back door.

I cry and insist I'll pay more attention in class, learn how to properly sing and dance, and listen to my elder sisters' teachings in the art of flirting.

"You were the one who always wanted to leave. This is your chance," the manager says as she rubs my back. "Crying to me now won't do you any good."

I leave that night, my actions keyed off my instinct to obey her every order. Hours after departing, I open the sack she gave me and find that underneath the tightly wrapped bao sit several ingots of gold, enough to purchase a house with enough land to start a farm. Not even my mother could've earned this much gold, even if her career as an elite courtesan continued until a proper retirement. I tear through a plain steamed mantou and continue walking. The manager told me not to stop until the main road completely faded from view and mountains submerged me, but so few people pass through this area, unless they come from the mountainside riding donkeys because horses cost them a lifetime's savings. I kick the stones in my path while counting the number of stray dogs I pass, skinny creatures with fur wrapping their ribs and snouts sharp like those of wolves.

As I wind around a group of dogs, careful to maintain my distance, I hear a clack of hooves and rumble of wheels over the dirt, the movement kicking up stones that clatter aside. The dogs scamper from the road, hiding behind trees and rocks. A fancy carriage surrounded by soldiers pulls up, each wooden side painted bright red and the windows covered by thin planks of wood patterned to form a maze of geometric shapes. I step off the road and onto the grass so it can pass and so I can take in the designs. There are intricate green and blue paintings of snakes at the top, red knots hanging and swaying from each corner,patterned silks that block the entrance, each fabric covered with calligraphy that I try to read as it nears. Instead of kicking up dirt in my face as it passes, the carriage stops where I stand and two hands emerge from behind the fabrics to pull them to the side. My father steps out of the carriage, his neat robes brushing the dirt ground. I stifle the instinct to bundle the silk together and dust it clean.

"If I'd known that woman would have sent you away the same night, I'd have retrieved you then and there," he sighs, extending a hand. "Do you plan to walk until you die of hunger and thirst? With me, you'll never lack anything."

I hesitate, staring at his fingers. "What about my mother? Why didn't you buy her out after she got pregnant?"

"I planned to," he answers. "But she became pregnant before I could complete the transaction. I can't take in a concubine after they fall pregnant. Too many questions about the legitimacy of the child. Very poorly timed and a shame—there was no one quite like your mother, not in the brothel, and not in the palace either."

"You could've just said she got pregnant after you took her in, couldn't you?"

My father shakes his head as though trying and failing to teach a young duckling to swim. "You could already see the bulge in her stomach. In the cinched waist-tight garments she wore, you'd only be able to fool a blind dog. But you are different. You're young. You have a future and an opportunity to grow in a better environment than a brothel. Why pass it up?"

From behind me, the stray dogs begin to growl as though they can smell the wealth exuding from this man and his well-fed flesh lacking sores and cracks. I spot one of the dogs' tails, tense and alert.

"I don't need any more than this," I say, lifting the bag the manager handed me.

"You don't know what's best for you at this age. That's understandable," my father begins. Two of the men patrolling the sides of the carriage grab my arms. I kick at their legs and try to knee their torsos, but a tough material encases their upper bodies and sends pangs of pain down my knee when I make contact. Their legs remain steadfast and immobile as though made of stone. I continue to kick anyway. The moment you stop fighting is when you lose, a lesson the manager drilled into all the girls' heads, even if some weren't destined to become courtesans. The men tie my hands behind my back with a long, silk sash, the knot so tight my fingers lose circulation. The more I try to pull my hands free, the tighter the knot draws, and I'm too much of a coward to dislocate my thumbs to escape the restraints.

"This isn't going to do you any good," I attempt to negotiate. "I'm useless. I can't cook or study well. I'm too weak for physical labor."

My father ignores me. "Put her in the carriage once she stops moving." The men wrestle a sack over my head as though I am a criminal rather than an estranged daughter. I hiss, baring my teeth and rearing my head as they grab the strands of my hair. I bite down on the hand holding the sack and the man yelps, dropping it to the floor. He clutches his hand, skin embedded with a curved row of teeth marks and specks of blood I also taste on my molars. The other man lunges toward me, grabbing at my neck and holding my head immobile.

The dogs scatter. A light padding grows louder, crunching the small leaves and rocks with each step. I spot the shadow first: a dark mass that spreads from one side of the road to the other, moving like waves over the earth. The two men pause their movements too, and I quickly wrench my head away and stumble to the ground, unable to break my fall with my tied hands. Each of the creature's tails curl and ripple, creating the shape of a restless, fluid fan.

The nine-tailed fox approaches at a constant pace, as though waiting for us to make a wrong step. It walks like it's dancing, the way my mother would sway and turn while holding ribbons billowing around her. Its mouth opens slightly, sharp teeth lining its jaw, tongue tasting the atmosphere as though our bodies' flavor is palpable from a distance. The fox's eyes reflect the sunlight, flecks of yellow and red burning around the dark slit pupil. I've never seen a fox so large before, and it suddenly seems reasonable that this creature devours disgraced courtesans whole.

The two men stand paralyzed while my father, mesmerized just moments ago, regains the momentum in his limbs and walks forward, his long robe drifting over the road behind him as though he too grew a tail he could flaunt.

"Great fox, return the courtesan you devoured to me," he proclaims, positioned just slightly out of the fox's tail-sweeping radius. "Return *all* of the courtesans' lives you unjustly consumed to satiate your greedy hunger."

The fox's tails continue to sway like nine snakes sizing up their prey. The edges of its mouth lift in an uncanny human-like smile, revealing the teeth that extend to the back of its jaw. The smile of a courtesan—one who has already opened her legs, body, and heart, stitched loosely back together. The fox is silent beyond the soft swooshes of wind combing between its tails and the thump from each paw hitting the ground, its seductive and drowning grin frozen on its face. My father cowers as the fox's shadow envelops his body, the sudden blockage of sunlight chilling the entire road. I shiver and attempt to stand up again, preparing to run. I half expect my father to run too, since no human stands a chance against a beast so large. Instead, he remains in one spot, shoulders hunched forward and head bent slightly, as though his arms could protect him from suffering the brunt of a blow. Despite his inability to make eye contact with the fox, he repeats, "Return the courtesans, else you are but a beast no more noble than the common stray dog."

The fox continues forward, and before I can register the crunch or the vibrations in the ground or my father's split-second lift of his chin or his delusional lovelorn gaze, the fox's paw crushes him into the ground like an insect, hard on the outside and a leaking host of flesh on the inside. The fox's movement doesn't slow. The other men rush to escape in the carriage and on the horses. It stops in front of me, my legs weak from hours of walking and prickly from the loss of circulation in my toppled state. I bow my head, close my eyes, and wait for it to stomp me into the ground too.

But instead, a gust tickles my neck and drifts down my back, gentle yet sharp, the kind of wind you get from slicing through the air with a knife. The knot around my wrists loosens and falls. I open my eyes and lift my arms, rubbing the red circles imprinted like cuffs on my skin. The nine-tailed fox has already passed me, continuing forth in the direction I came from, hours along an increasingly straight road that reaches the brothel, where luxury and temptation meet business transactions and perhaps the discreet courtesan trying to toss her newborn child down a well. I sit behind a rock, hidden from the dogs that have gathered around my father's remains, grateful for the wind blowing the scent of blood away from me. I wait until the fox's tails disappear into the horizon, waving nine final goodbyes.

threads and crossings

Poetry Collection

Joy Pepito

Joy Pepito

Roots of a Foreign Stitch

I am the foreign stitch
in the fabric of a homeland left behind,
a voice adrift in foreign cadence,
my tongue halting over *po* and *opo*,
hands raised for *mano*,
symbols weighty and fragile,
like heirlooms carried oceans away.

Here,
in the land where I am both guest and stranger,
the air smells of streets I do not know,
its hymns foreign, its sunlight thinner—
I stumble,
my steps echoing the rhythm of archipelagos
that sleep in the marrow of my bones.
Misunderstanding builds its scaffolds high,
planks of judgment, nails of silence,
walls that do not yield
to the whispers of exile,
to the prayer of belonging.

I am not forgetful—
not of shores where *amihan* kissed my skin,
not of rice fields, heavy with song—
but here, my gestures falter,
my reverence misunderstood,
a mirror of culture cracked in transit.
The divide grows deeper,
a gulf swollen with histories unspoken,
and still, I reach,
my heart, a *bahay kubo* perched on fragile stilts,

rooted in islands that call me *anak*,
even as I wander distant,
distant shores.

The Supper Hour

At the long table, lacquered with years,
she perches—a ghost pinned in the candlelight,
her silence brittle as frost on bone china.
The elders speak, their words, a caravan
of sermons and certainties, trampling her voice—
a flicker doused in the gale of tradition.

How sharp the weight of reverence,
its edges cutting the tongue that longs to rebel.
Her thoughts, barbed and restless,
skitter like trapped sparrows,
wingbeats swallowed in the heavy vault
of their unlistening ears.

The ritual unfolds,
forks clinking like bells tolling her restraint,
laughter rising hollow and bright,
masking the cavern of her unspoken grief.
To shatter their sanctum with anger—
no, that would be treason,
a sin carved deep into the family ledger.

They think they know her,
her heart wrapped tight in their creased blueprints,
but they map only the surface,

the fragile carapace she learned to wear.
Beneath lies an ocean of unsaid storms,
unwept tears,
the ache of communion unmet.

Respect is her armor, her disguise,
polished, but brittle as tarnished silver.
She wears it well,
though it smothers her pulse,
makes a crypt of the supper hour.
And as the plates empty,
the candles gutter low,
she drifts deeper into herself—
a phantom among the living,
her solitude echoing in the silent hollow of her chest.

The Children of Endless Crossings

We are the children of endless crossings,
our names like ghosts,
whispers tossed into foreign winds,
echoes that never quite return.
At home, they ask for silence,
but it is a silence soaked in expectation,
like the earth beneath your feet,
quiet, but laden with unspoken demands—
to be everything
and nothing all at once.

In the land of your birth,
you are the shadow that doesn't quite belong—
neither the first nor the last
to stand with trembling hands,
half-formed and divided,
split between two skies,
each too heavy to lift.

They want you to hold them all—
the weight of their sorrow, their pride,
but you—
you are a thread pulled too tight,
a stitch undone,
tearing at the edges,
fraying where the seams should hold.

In the mirror,
your reflection is an answer
you cannot give.
You are the child of all that is
and all that could never be—
always caught between the smell of incense
and the taste of salt in the air.

At night, you are the quiet hum of the earth,
but under the weight of their desires,
you are nothing but a song forgotten,
straining to be heard,
drowning in your own half-formed words,
a bridge built with no intention of crossing.

Joy Pepito

And still,
you dance between two worlds,
one foot in each,
but no place to stand.
Tethered to an ancestry that asks for more,
and a future that expects everything,
you walk the line of the impossible—
the third child of the first,
the lost child of a place you've never known.

The day will come,
and you will bend
under the weight of your own bones—
a child forever unmade,
a promise forever broken.

Silence
Between Us Raised Me

Poetry Collection

Hannan Khan

Silence Between Us Raised Me

(he) reluctantly opened his mouth—
     (as if) really to say something… something important
     but the words (caught) between his teeth
     like charred meat heavily stuck after dinner
     (so i desperately waited) watching his jaw shift
     but nothing (except a silent sigh) came out

his lips (stayed shut)
     like an organized cupboard of unworn shirts
     lingering lexicons buttoned up—austere
     (so i slowly learned to iron muteness
     to crease my questions
     to press my whispers into crisp, forgettable lines)

(son) he calmly called me
     (but only when) i had scrapped my knees
     when my tappers (bled) from clutching football air
     schoolyard clinging dust
     (broken bicycles, broken promises, broken utterances)
     (when my report card) lounged on a vintage table
     in principal's office
               his sunken eyes skimmed over it
               like a littered newspaper headline
     (adoring acknowledgement was a luxury
               praise an afterthought)

his boisterous voice (was a receipt)
     precisely folded small in his pocket
     proof of something bought (but never fully given)
     (it crumpled roughly) when he rashly reached for his keys
     when he quickly fished out loose change
     when he paid for things he thought mattered more

he taught me (how to drive)
        (handed me) the steering wheel
        with a hushedness that buckled me in
        (tutored me to read a map) but never directions to him
        (he sat in the passenger seat)
        diligently correcting my turns
        my speed
        my wavering hesitation
        but never my uncrossable distance from him

(he never) said goodbye
        (he never) said sorry
        (he never) said stay
        (so i mastered) leaving was always easier than explaining
        (so i packed my bags) in quietude
        folded my camicie like unfinished conversations
        languidly left the porch light on
                (in case) he utterly wanted to follow

when i said (father, tell me)
        he gently cleared his throat (as if)
        he might say something actually
        (but exited the room instead)
        (i listened) to the echoing sounds of his footsteps
        to the polished door sighing shut
        to the quiet that settled (like ash in an empty chair)

(i am) older now
        (i speak) in parenthesis too
        when my naughty son asks
        (i lovingly hold his palm)
        (i ardently say the vocables)
        even when they bitterly taste like a rusted iron
        even when they oxidize in my oral cavity
        even when they ruthlessly choke me on their way out

(because silence) is a lethal inheritance
(one that thickens blood
        locks kisser and grips throats)
(so i blatantly break it
      splinter it
        shatter it to filth)
(i pristinely place expressions) into my son's hands
not like inherited heirloom, but like fervent fire
(something) to warm him
      to burn away the frozen cold
to remind him (always)
    that love is meant to be softly and sweetly spoken

Somewhere A Girl Will See Herself Disappear

the first rosy night—she peels gold from her fragile wrist
gently unclasps glossy pearls from her throat
flowers in her snaky braid wilt before she touches them
enchanting jasmine crumbles between her fingers
alluring scent, heavy suffocating
"you'll easily get used to it," he says,
seductively watching her from the bed
"to what?" she asks, hushed voice tightly caught
between old promises and new silences.
"... to all of it."
she turns to the mirror
searching for the confident girl who should answer, but

finds only the heft of his words instantly settling on her shoulders
she peeks herself in the reflector—not a blessed bride
not a bold girl
the baked bangles on the dresser do not sing
the veil on the chair doesn't move
her blushing face is hers

but the intoxicating eyes are someone else's

the hazed morning after,
the house is a spotlight stage, truly set before she arrives
she enters like a guest overstaying the warm welcome
howling eyes weigh her — slice her
count her worth in gold bracelets
closely measure her muteness like it's an heirloom
passed down generations
the mother-in-law diligently teaches her the home science of
shrinking — smaller voice
smaller steps
smaller dreams
subtly perfecting the art of disappearing
between stove flames and duty.
the father-in-law doesn't speak but dictates in glances
 a woman is respect
he quietly says without words and respect is what folds hands
lower gaze
respect doesn't question
doesn't deny
doesn't demand.
the sister-in-law scans from the dusky doorway
bittersweet smiles like warnings
hands that push — a hushed competition
a never-ending game of who bends
further? who breaks softer?
who disappears first?

the dewar calls her *bhabi* with a smirk
with blinks that linger half a second too long
a brother-in-law by name — a stranger in moments stolen
she laughs too little
talks too calculated
for a lexeme misheard is a keen knife to her throat
the walls listen — the susurrations grow
 a jolly joke, an adoring gaze
a fervent gasp out of place and suddenly

she's something unspeakable
her shadow, next to his, is a scandal
her quietude around him is
a sinister confession
she learns that even absence is presence
and innocence is something she cannot prove — ever.

the hearty husband was a mellow spoken
before the sacred wedding
now utters in unfinished sentences
unfinished love that never reaches
the void space between them
sable night squashes against her chest
dreamy days stretch without name — without shape
she is the daughter who no longer belongs at home
and the wife who still stands at the threshold
neither here nor there
a misplaced belonging

icy morning is the weight of tea tray
no sugar for herself — just for elders
her digits learn to serve before they learn to hold
drowning evening is hot seat at the table where love is portioned
where she eats last
where her hunger is not hers, but a service
a compelling proof — a destined duty
haunted years blur in cotton fabric of her dupatta
worn
washed
reworn
faded
an obscured testimony no one reads
until one long day—
she does not wake up before the entire house
she doesn't make the steaming tea
she doesn't lower her longing gaze

she gracefully walks out — barefoot
no keys, no explanations, no note left behind
just the familiar sound of her pant
unshackled for the first time
the chained walls do not crack
the engulfing floors do not swallow her
the sapphire sky doesn't turn onyx
they'll say, "she was irresponsibly reckless"
they will say, " she was genuinely ungrateful"
they will say, " she never belonged"
long after the house slowly stops whispering her name
and long after they rewrite her into lull
somewhere a girl will press her haggard palms

against the same illusory mirror.

Urdu Bazar: A Love Letter No One Reads Anymore

*(for the historic city, for the majestic bazar, for the paperbacks we forget
to return)*

spined along the southern walls of the Badshahi Mosque
where the air is dense with musk and nostalgic bibliosmia
of old paper. here booksellers lavishly drink chai in
porcelain cups stained with the clinging dust of
timeless centuries. their fingernails rimmed
with the soot from first editions—
their breath laced with the
scent of burnt
newspapers

signboard above the doorway in the bazar is older than the
ash choking streets, older than the cassette–tape vendor
two shops down who still sells Mehdi Hassan's voice
to wind older than the boy swiftly frying samosas
in reused oil — his hands slick with history and
yesterday wages. shopfront is a crumbling
ghazal, script peeling like last pages of
forgotten masnavi – reads " مکتبِ عشق,"
"Bookstore of Love" letters
calligraphy half–erased
by monsoon rot

step inside: here aroma is rich with rust of urdu typewriters
ink dissolving into time, pages swollen with Lahore's
breath; smell of rain–fattened paper, of moth–bitten
nostalgia. the street writhes with bodies — PU and
Ravians haggling over guidebooks poets
running their fingers on the ghosts of
out–of–print ghazals, clerks
hunting for pocket–size
Masnavi–e–Rumi—
a thousand salted
hands thumbing
through pages
without
buying

their voices tangled in the radio static of the shop playing
Noor Jehan from audio–tapes older than the shopkeeper
himself. and this is — this is Urdu Bazar, where —
pamphlets were once printed in secret, where a
torn Dastan–E–Amir Hamza could be read
by candlelight with the window shut…
where Faiz once walked, where
Manto once cursed… where
poets once whispered the
revolution into the ears
of typewriters

step inside… step inside, where the world slows to sound of
pages turning, where light seeps through wooden rafters
like forgotten verses. you'll find here: a tattered Toba
Tek Singh, its last page missing… spine cracked in
two — Manto's insanity unfinished his final
sentence an open wound — somewhere
Saadat Hasssan Manto exhales…
a leather bound Ghalib with
a pressed marigold
between pages
113 and 114

a secondhand copy of Dast–e–Saba (handwriting in margins
'Faiz tera sheher bohat ajnabi lagta hai'): for Majeed
who dreams of Balkh and Bukhara but wakes to the
sound of load–shedding — a 1952 edition of
Angaray, its edges burnt, its words once
illegal, still smoldering in the memory
of a bookseller who watched the
police cart away volumes
like they were
contraband
flesh

bookseller sits hunched behind the counter — white beard
veined with the dirt — knows every book's weight in
centuries… knows which ones were smuggled
which ones were banned… which ones were
disappeared. he coughs in the back room
where literary meetings still coil in
wooden shelves — smoke from
an old… capstan cigarette
curling between
yellowing
pages of
Lihaf

he doesn't look up when you ask for Basti. he doesn't look
up when you ask for Thanda Gosht (cold meat). he only
sighs, heavy as the weight of unsold books pressed
against the walls… and tells you that these books
the ones that mattered… don't come anymore
the ones in circulation are hoarded, locked
in glass cabinets, turned into collector's
items for those who care about pages
but not about words. he gestures
to the shelves — they are still
books. but they're new
they're hollow

you grab a pristine hardcover; its gold lettering untouched
by time. it is a book of poems by a man who doesn't
read poetry. a novel about Lahore written by a
novelist who has never walked its bustling
streets of Anarkali. a history rewritten
so many times, it is now only
scaffolding, striped
of fossil bones
striped of
truth

the shop is dying… outside the street is alive
the bookseller doesn't ask you to buy
anything. he only asks — without
words — if you'll remember
this place when it is gone
then he turns away…
back to his desk…
back to his classic
books…
back to his
ashes

Chang E

Ling Yuan

Numbers, numbers, numbers. Another lunar eclipse to calculate, another cycle to track. You'd think being the Moon Goddess would be more... glamorous. But no, it's all formulas and admin work here. And my only company? A rice-cake-pounding rabbit. I've tried requesting more staff, you know—qualified mathematicians. But every time I petition the Queen Mother of the West, she just sighs dramatically and points at some gloomy clouds. "This isn't the time to expand your office," she says. As if clouds are an acceptable excuse for denying a headcount.

No one has time for the moon these days. Down there it's all chaos. Have you seen what the other departments are handling? God of Wealth goes viral with cryptocurrency lectures and the God of Longevity is forever battling the endless flu situation. I envy them, I'll admit. They get all the glory on earth—the perfumed incense, lit candles, and sweet-smelling flowers. It's no wonder their subordinates stand taller and glow brighter. The Pottery God and I should start a support group.

But then I think about those pointless meetings, those work lunches full of fake laughter and petty gossip... no, it's better here with my abacus and rabbit. The poets still write about me, don't they? Let the God of Wealth have his Bitcoin; I have sonnets.

Only during the Mid-Autumn Festival do they remember me. Those precious nights when mortals gather with their lanterns, faces turned skyward to admire my handiwork. If only they knew what really goes on up here.

I suppose I should address the elephant in the room—or should I say, the elixir in the room? Everyone down there thinks they know my story. "Chang E, the thief who stole from her hero husband Hou Yi." Please. I may have had a drinking problem back then but a thief? Never. How was I supposed to know the bottle wasn't just another of his hidden wine stash but the elixir of immortality bestowed on him by the Queen Mother as a reward for shooting down nine suns from the sky and saving earth from scorching to ashes? Really, who leaves something like that under a pillow without so much as a label?

I can still remember the shock of that moment: our house suddenly beneath my feet, my body floating past clouds and into space until I landed on this rock. One hundred years it took me to master all these lunar formulas and heavenly protocols after I accidentally ascended. One hundred years! No orientation, no training, just "Congratulations, you're the Moon Goddess now!" and a stack of instruction manuals dumped on me by the Heavenly Minister of Celestial Appointments. What choice did I have?

And so, I'm stuck here wading in a sea of numbers, wondering when it will all end. After every soul reaches nirvana and the earthly realm ceases to exist, where will we go next? Even the highest gods don't know that one. But the day I sign off my last calculation and get off this rock, I will look for Hou Yi and tell him this: it wasn't betrayal, just a very poorly placed elixir.

Sohwakhaeng

Rena Johnson

Rena Johnson

The snow falls in thick, downy clumps, miniature clouds drifting down from the bleached sky. Two birds chirp and twitter from a nearby grandfather oak; their lemon-bright duet floats through the muffled silence of the snowfall.

White blanches the landscape, softening the ground and blurring the horizon. My feet are still toasty from the *ondol* floor, the heat of the furnace following my every footstep through the snow like a warm shadow.

The world is quiet here, and I think my mom is right—the snowflakes in Korea are bigger, fluffier, than they are in America. The morning stretches from mountaintop to mountaintop, and I can see the edges of it curling past the peaks of the earth, shades of pink and gold blushing behind fingers of white.

Only a couple of months ago, the mountains were green and vital, the valley a bowl of fertile crops and sunlit pastures. I remember the way the sun stroked the earth, planes of gold cutting across the mountains, a patchwork of light and shadow overlaying the vast slopes.

Now, the mountains sleep, as does the rest of the valley. Only the birds and I seem to be awake for the first snow.

I do not yet know that in order to find the rest of my mom's long-lost family, she will have to face a man whom she contemplates killing for what he did when she was young. I do not yet know that when we finally find her mother's grave, she will fall to her knees and cry, and I, in my limited knowledge of the language, will only be able to understand the first word she tentatively sobs: *mianhae*—I'm sorry.

I do not yet know the meanings of the words *han* and *jeong*. *Han*—the word to describe the deep, unrelenting sorrow and rage for having suffered unjustly. *Jeong*—the word to describe the deep, unrelenting love and compassion for kith and kin.

These words are as ingrained in the country as the mountains that surround me—mountains so prevalent that it is impossible to stand on Korean soil and see a horizon untouched by them. Silent witnesses to the endurance of humanity: the sins of the father, the love of the child, all cradled in the ancient hands of a land that was here far longer than us, and will prevail long after the last human memory fades.

But while humans persist, *han* and *jeong* permeate our histories, two words spoken by only one percent of the world, and yet they echo out, the words losing shape and form, but felt just as deeply. As the mountains the world over know the chill of winter and the warmth of spring, our bones know the ache of grief and the lightness of love.

The last word that I do not yet know is *sohwakhaeng*—small but certain happiness. A cup of coffee, or curling up with a book next to a warm window. The curl of a new leaf, a dog playing in fresh snow. The quiet of a peaceful morning as the rest of the world sleeps. The knowledge that, no matter what has happened in the past or what will happen in the future, the birds will continue to sing to each other, and *ondol* floors will continue to warm soles.

I stand and watch the snow float down from the sky. The world is simpler like this. Quiet, in shades of white and gray. I do not yet know what the future will hold, but for this moment, I tilt my face toward the sky. The heavens are hazy and the birdsong bright, and as the world sleeps, I let myself feel like a child again. I open my mouth and catch a snowflake on my tongue.

Meet the Authors

O. Hunt

Grand Prize Winner: *Meena*

O. Hunt, the grand-prize winner of the inaugural *Winds of Asia* award was born and raised in India. She currently lives with her husband in Mississauga, Canada, and is focusing on writing fiction after a season of freelance work. Fiction, she explains, enriches her inner life by helping her expand on thoughts and emotions that are otherwise difficult to realize outside of written, narrative form. She hopes something in her work makes the reader remember it long after they finish it. When she isn't writing, she can be found exploring the outdoors, dream journaling, enjoying anime or podcasts, or reading.

Lam Ho

1st Runner Up: *Amerasian*

Lam Ho is a communications professional and climate action advocate from the Southeastern United States. A graduate of Sewanee: The University of the South with degrees in English and Environment & Sustainability, she draws inspiration from her travels, romantic experiences, and her immigrant parents' stories to craft poetry, essays, and fiction. She performs spoken word poetry and is currently writing her first novel. Lam lives with her mildly famous cat, Jose.

Jade Mah-Vierling

2nd Runner Up: *The Salted Fish Turns Over*

Jade Mah-Vierling holds a B.A. in English Literature from the University of British Columbia and an M.A. from the University of Calgary, where her thesis explored mixed-race identity in life writing genres such as biotext, memoir, and documentary. She now writes speculative fiction centered on Asian and mixed-race themes. Based in Calgary, Alberta, Jade works as a freelance marketer and editor at OnSpec magazine, sharing her home with her husband and crazy dog.

Alex Van Huynh
Death in the Daylilies

Dr. Alex Van Huynh earned his Ph.D. in Biology from Lehigh University and serves as an Assistant Professor of Biology at DeSales University in Center Valley, Pennsylvania. His research explores diverse questions in ecology, evolution, and conservation. Beyond the lab, his poetry appears in numerous literary journals, reflecting a deep curiosity about the natural world and human experience. His debut full-length poetry collection, Inquiry, was published in 2023.

Anna Li Stollman
Mycelium

Anna Li Stollman is an emerging writer and international adoptee born in Chenzhou, China. Brought to America at ten months old, she grew up with her nose in a book and a cup of tea nearby. A practicing Buddhist, she enjoys scolding her cats and studying her mother tongue. Anna currently lives in Pennsylvania, where she studies anthropology and creative writing at the University of Pittsburgh and teaches at an early learning center.

Anton Imbong
Swirlings

Anton Imbong is a Filipino writer pursuing a master's degree in the Humanities at the University of Asia and the Pacific. A storyteller at heart, he explores writing through playscripts, Asian literature, and poetry. His goals include becoming an established spoken word artist and publishing a poetry collection inspired by Ocean Vuong. He is currently completing his master's thesis on local spoken word communities in Metro Manila, reflecting his passion for language and performance.

Aparna Rajan
Inheritance

Aparna R is a Ph.D. research scholar, freelance copyeditor, and translator between Malayalam and English. She holds an M.A. and M.Phil. in English and resides in Kerala, India. Her micro fiction "On Loving" was published in A Story in 100 Words. Passionate about exploring imagination through language, she enjoys writing speculative and fantasy fiction, as well as experimenting with short prose forms such as flash fiction and micro narratives.

Cathy Millangue
Of Those Who Lived and Died

Cathy Millangue is a Filipino-American high school student living in Missouri. Her favorite subjects are History and Orchestra, where she plays the violin. An avid fan of fantasy, superheroes, and video games like Assassin's Creed, Baldur's Gate III, and Marvel Rivals, she also enjoys drawing, writing, and reading. Passionate about creativity and science, Cathy hopes to become a green architect or geneticist, write a book, travel abroad, and learn a new language.

Connie Chen
餃子 *JiaoZi (Dumplings)*

Connie Chen is a nonfiction writer and visual artist exploring divinity within objected, abjected, and rejected bodies. A Master of Divinity graduate from Harvard, where she studied religion and literature, her work has appeared in The Flannery O'Connor Review and is forthcoming on America's Test Kitchen's Proof podcast. She is pursuing an MFA in creative nonfiction at the University of Iowa as an Iowa Arts Fellow and is one of fourteen recognized Master Penmen worldwide.

Dea Ratna
Urang Sunda

Dea Ratna is a writer and artist based in Jakarta, Indonesia. They hold a Diploma in Fine Art from the Nanyang Academy of Fine Arts in Singapore and work as a freelance writer. Their essays often explore art, identity, and intersectionality, with occasional ventures into short fiction. Dea's work has appeared in Into the Spine, Artgence, and X Marks the Spot. They live with two cats and enjoy playing video games in their free time.

Diane Yang
Elegies of Nanjing

Diane Yang is a queer writer and artist based in Shanghai, China. A graduate of NYU's Tisch School of the Arts, she developed a voice exploring the intersections of Asian and queer identities. Her work examines the fluidity of self, the weight of Chinese cultural trauma, and the reconstruction of identity amid social and political pressures. After four years in Brooklyn, she continues to create art that bridges personal experience and collective memory.

Elina Kumra
Ontology of Water Memory

Elina Kumra is a BIPOC writer from California. Her work appears in Kinsman Quarterly's *Black Butterfly* collection and explores themes of nature, identity, and renewal. Blending introspection with lyricism, Elina writes to uncover the quiet beauty within transformation. When she isn't writing, she enjoys naming raindrops and observing the poetry of the everyday, bringing sensitivity and imagination to all she creates.

Farah Art Griffin
my name is Farah

Farah Art Griffin's poetry has appeared or is forthcoming in Pleiades, The American Journal of Poetry, Arkansas Review, Good River Review, Constellations, and Storm Cellar, among others. Her work was featured in the North Dakota Human Rights Arts Festival. Recipient of the Altman Writers of Color Scholarship from the Hudson Valley Writers Center and a grant from the Writers Happiness Movement, Farah holds an Ed.M. in Arts in Education from Harvard University and resides in California.

Hannan Khan
Silence Between Us Raised Me

Hannan Khan is a poet and scholar of literature and linguistics from Pakistan. His work traverses love, loss, and the unseen spaces between—merging ghazal and haibun, intimacy and apocalypse. His writing has appeared in Failed Haiku, IHRAM Literary Magazine, and SpecPoVerse, with more forthcoming from Graveside Press. Through language, Hannan explores the delicate tension between what is breathed and what remains unspoken, crafting poetry that lingers at the edge of spirit and sound.

Hasanah Mishahal Mansour
Dearest Floodplain Mother

Hasanah is a writer and college student pursuing a B.S. in Accountancy in the Philippines. Writing has been her passion since childhood, a flame woven into her being. She is currently developing her debut collection, aiming to inspire others through stories that stir emotion and reveal quiet truths. Her essays express the storms within her, capturing resilience and reflection. For Hasanah, writing is not a pastime—it is a calling, a fire that endures.

Jiang Pu
Touch

Jiang Pu is a first-generation Chinese American author and Ed leader. Her recent poems have appeared in California Quarterly, Catamaran, Panorama (U.K.), among others, and in several anthologies. She holds a Ph.D. in Education from Michigan State University, and is the founder of NextGen Education. She grows a bee & butterfly garden in the San Francisco Bay Area of California. Her first name means "a big river". Find her at www.jiangpu.org.

Jocelyn A Chin
Last Train Home

Jocelyn A. Chin is a high school humanities teacher based in Cleveland, Ohio. She studied public policy, philosophy, education, and creative writing at Duke University, where she cultivated her passion for storytelling and social inquiry. A devoted runner and rock climber, she often draws creative inspiration from the endurance and mindfulness these pursuits demand. Her poetry and flash nonfiction explore connections between nature, community, and belonging—guiding her continually back to others and to herself.

Joy Pepito
threads and crossings

Joy Pepito is a writer based in Metro Manila, Philippines. She works as a copywriter, spending most of her time trying to make words behave. She writes contemporary fiction about mental health, messy families, and all the quiet, complicated moments in between. When she's not working, she's romanticizing slow mornings or jotting down story ideas of which she'll pretend weren't inspired by real life. For more about Joy's upcoming book, follow her on Instagram @joy.pepito_.

Karina Cheah
The Spaces Inside

Karina Cheah grew up in Bethesda, Maryland in a multicultural Southeast Asian household. She earned an MA in Biography and Creative Non-Fiction from the University of East Anglia and a BA in International Relations from Colgate University. She has published a short story collection, This Side of the Veil. Her nonfiction work appears in print in the anthology Creative Non-Fiction from Egg Box Publishing and Welter Issue 58, and online on New Writing and The Masters Review.

KC Sisomphone
i40

KC Sisomphone is writer and educator from the United States. Originally from Greensboro, North Carolina, he earned his BS and MA from Appalachian State University and has taught throughout North Carolina. He writes poetry and essays that center around themes of place, identity, and spirituality. When he's not writing, he loves to cook, walk his dog, and watch way too much television. He currently lives and writes in Wilmington, North Carolina, where he also works as a pre-college advisor.

Ling Yuan
Chang E

Ling Yuan's fiction has been shortlisted for the Chautauqua Janus Prize and the Black Warrior Review Fiction Prize. Her short stories have appeared or are forthcoming in the minnesota review, Grattan Street Press, Crannog, and elsewhere. Living in Singapore, she writes about memory, displacement, and the quiet intersections between identity and belonging. Ling is currently at work on her first novel, which explores the emotional landscapes that shape human connection.

Linh Truong
Toxic

Linh Truong is a second-generation Vietnamese immigrant, born and raised in the Californian Bay Area where she still resides. She majored in Literature at the University of California, Santa Cruz and was accepted into the Creative Writing Concentration before promptly dropping out. Her writing often focuses on Asian history and the Asian-American experience through the lens of romance. She enjoys good stories, traveling, boba tea, sunny days, driving fast, and even, on occasion, writing.

Lucy Zhang
Art of a Courtesan

Lucy Zhang writes, codes, and watches anime. Her work has appeared in Virginia Quarterly Review, Shenandoah, The Massachusetts Review, and other journals. Blending her background in technology with storytelling, she explores intersections of the digital and the deeply human, where logic meets emotion. When she isn't writing, she's probably debugging code or finding inspiration in animated worlds. Find her at lucyzhang.tech or on Twitter (X) @Dango_Ramen

Michelle Chen
Beaut

Michelle Chen was born in Singapore and lives in New York City. She has attended multiple writing retreats, including the Iowa Young Writers' Studio. Her awards include the Best Masters Essay Prize, PhD Works Awards for Career Exploration, and the AAPI Mentorship Network Travel Grant, and thoroughly enjoys observing in high-need schools, making literary criticism exciting, adventuring across time and space with chill professors, and getting less ice and less sugar in her winter melon milk tea.

Mir Aziz
Goat Screams

Mir Aziz is a British Pakistani writer whose work explores the intersections of religion, philosophy, and human emotion. Rooted in the highlands of modern Pakistan, his stories draw on the region's rich mythology, history, and culture to illuminate the beauty and tragedy of existence. Through his writing, Mir examines the tensions between faith and doubt, tradition and modernity. His previous work, "Shadows on the Frontier," delves into the philosophy of conflict and moral complexity..

Stock photos are used for authors who prefer anonymity.

Rena Johnson
Sohwakhaeng

Rena Johnson was born and raised in the American Midwest, but she ventured to the east coast to graduate from NYU's Tisch School of the Arts with a bachelor's in Cinema Studies. She currently works in education, but when she isn't being taught teenage slang by her students, she can usually be found writing, reading, and watching speculative fiction, playing tabletop and video game RPGs, or practicing kendo. Her hope when writing is to foster empathy, understanding, and connection.

Rishabh Motwani
Coup

Rishabh Motwani is a poet and writer based in India. An MBA graduate and valedictorian, he currently runs a pharmaceutical business while pursuing his passion for storytelling. His work spans poetry, short fiction, and drama, exploring the intricacies of human emotion and memory. Fascinated by dreams and déjà vu, Rishabh draws inspiration from surreal experiences that shape the lyrical and introspective nature of his writing. He is equally drawn to cinema and visual storytelling.

Sandra Jackson-Opoku
Big River Crossing and Dirty Dozens

Sandra Jackson-Opoku is the African-American author of two novels, and the recipient of a National Endowment for the Arts Fellowship, the American Library Association Black Caucus Award, a Chicago Esteemed Artist Award, a James Baldwin Fellowship at MacDowell Arts, and others. She is working on Black Rice, a historical novel inspired by family lore of a Chinese ancestor in 19th century Mississippi. A former professor of writing and literature, she presents readings and workshops across the country and worldwide.

Serrina Zou
Daughter Diaspora

Serrina Zou is a recent graduate of Columbia University with a BA in Creative Writing and Sociology. Her poetry and prose have been recognized internationally by the Bridport Poetry Prize, the Alpine Fellowship Poetry Prize, the Poetry Society of the U.K., the Robert and Adele Schiff Award in Poetry, among others. She has been nominated for the 2022 Pushcart Prize and Best Microfictions 2023. Outside of writing, Serrina adores Philz Coffee, long walks with friends, discovering independent bookstores, inventing new recipes for baked treats, and mid-afternoon naps.

Sol Zerrudo
Kaingin

Sol Zerrudo is a Filipino interactive fiction writer and game designer. A descendant of the Panay Bukidnon tribe, she explores the enduring scars of colonialism, the desecration of culture, and the resilience that grows from loss. Through her immersive narratives, she seeks to preserve indigenous memory and voice within modern storytelling forms. When not writing, Sol enjoys quiet mornings with coffee and croissants, dreaming of worlds where myth and resistance intertwine.

Songyee Park
A Dead Man's Bucket List

Songyee Park is a Korean writer and software developer based in Bangkok. Her fiction blends speculative imagination with folkloric depth, exploring memory, displacement, and the haunting beauty of liminal spaces. A translator of Korean webtoons into English, she bridges languages and worlds through story. Songyee will begin her studies in creative writing at the University of Oxford in late 2025. Her work reflects curiosity for the unseen and empathy for the in-between.

Tara Lall
lucky girl

Tara Lall is a recent graduate of UWC Costa Rica and an incoming student at the University of Edinburgh. Growing up among diverse cultures has deeply shaped her artistic voice and curiosity about identity and connection. An aspiring author, dancer, and multidisciplinary artist, she seeks to tell stories that move between cultures and art forms. Through writing and movement, Tara explores belonging, transformation, and the universal rhythms that tie people together.

Vaswati Das
For My Mother Who Learned to Smile in a Foreign Language

Vaswati Das was uprooted from the lush hills of Northeast India and replanted in the concrete sprawl of urban life, where she now works as a self-described "corporate photosynthesizer." Her poetry documents the chaos of childhood, the working-class inheritance of survival, and the silent violences of womanhood in India. She began writing at six—when children notice everything and adults look away. Vaswati's voice insists: *I'm here, I'm watching, and I have a pen.*

Zoe Parrott
The Hot and Cold Place

Zoe Parrott is an undergraduate student in the United States who writes opinion pieces, free-verse poetry, and short fiction. Her work often reflects on the intersections of emotion, nature, and self-discovery. She hopes to publish a book one day and continues to hone her craft through study and exploration. Outside of writing, Zoe enjoys gardening, singing, and spending time with her cat, finding creativity in the quiet details of everyday life.

Stock photos are used for authors who prefer anonymity.